BREATHE IN

NIKI ROBINSON-AGUE

1

PROLOGUE
The Overlook
New Zealand — Present Day

The wind at the edge of the world tasted like salt and beginning.

She stood at the cliff's edge, close enough that the updraft caught her hair and lifted it behind her like something being released. Below, the Tasman Sea threw itself against ancient rock, patient and relentless, reshaping the land one wave at a time. She'd always loved the ocean. The way it never stopped moving. The way it could wear down anything, given enough time.

The studio had opened three weeks ago. Soft Landing, she'd named it. The space was modest: polished concrete floors, white walls, windows that faced the harbor. Nothing like what she'd had before. But that was the point, wasn't it? Sometimes you had to let go of everything to find out what actually mattered.

She closed her eyes and let the wind scour her face.

It had been a hard year. The hardest of her life, maybe.

Losing the business. Losing her sister. Losing the version of herself she'd spent two decades building. There were days she wasn't sure she'd survive it—days when the grief felt like drowning, like being pulled under by something she couldn't see.

But she had survived. She was here. Standing at the edge of the world with salt on her lips and a second chance she hadn't expected.

That was the thing about yoga, about practice, about all of it. People thought it was about holding on—holding poses, holding your breath, holding yourself together. But the real teaching was in the release. In the surrender. In trusting that when you let go of who you were, something new would rise to meet you.

She opened her eyes. Breathed in. Breathed out.

Her phone buzzed in her pocket. A text from her new landlord confirming the cottage was ready. A reminder that her first class was tomorrow morning, 6 AM, four students signed up.

Four students. She smiled. She'd once taught classes of two hundred. Had waiting lists that stretched for years. Had people fly across oceans just to practice in her presence.

Four students felt like freedom.

She turned away from the cliff and walked back toward the coastal path, toward the small town where no one knew her history, toward the life she was slowly, carefully building from the wreckage of the old one.

She'd been many things in her forty-three years—daughter, sister, teacher, builder of small empires. She'd been lost and found and lost again. She'd made mistakes she couldn't undo and carried grief she couldn't name.

But here, now, with the salt wind in her hair and tomorrow waiting like an open door, she felt something she hadn't felt in a long time.

Hope.

The sun was setting over the harbor, painting the water in shades of copper and gold. She passed a couple walking a dog, smiled at them, received their smiles in return. Just a woman out for an evening walk. Just a yoga teacher starting over.

She let herself into her rented cottage, locked the door behind her, and stood for a moment in the quiet. The space was small but clean—a bed, a kitchen, a bathroom with a window that faced the sea. Enough. More than enough.

She showered, washing the salt from her skin, then wrapped herself in a towel and wiped the fog from the bathroom mirror.

The face that looked back was tired. Older than she remembered, though she supposed that was true for everyone. There were lines around her eyes now, a softness in her jaw that hadn't been there before. She looked like someone who had been through something.

She had.

"Okay," she said to her reflection. A promise. A prayer. "Let's see what happens next."

She turned off the light and walked to bed, leaving wet footprints on the floor that would be gone by morning.

Tomorrow, she would teach again. Tomorrow, she would begin again.

Tomorrow, everything would be different.

2

Mira
The Soft One

The room smelled like sandalwood and silence.

Mira moved through her apartment the way she always did —quietly, deliberately, like a woman who had learned long ago that stillness was its own kind of power. The space was small but intentional: white walls, uncluttered surfaces, a single orchid on the windowsill that she'd kept alive for three years through careful attention. No art on the walls. No photographs. Nothing that announced who she was or where she'd been.

She preferred it this way. Clean. Contained. A life with no excess.

The afternoon light was fading, going amber and soft through the sheer curtains. She had two hours before her class —plenty of time to prepare, to settle into herself, to become what her students needed her to be.

She showered slowly, letting the hot water unknot her shoulders. Then she stood in front of the bathroom mirror, watching the steam curl and dissipate, watching her own face emerge from the fog.

Same face as her sister. Same dark eyes, same cheekbones, same full mouth. People always marveled at how identical they looked—*thats the thing about identical twins*. But Mira knew the differences. She saw them every time she looked in the mirror. Something in the expression. Something in the eyes. Maya's face was always performing, always projecting warmth and charisma outward like a searchlight. Mira's face was a door that stayed closed.

She let her hair air-dry, watching it settle into its natural waves. Maya always wore her hair pulled back—sleek ponytails, tight buns, every strand controlled. Mira couldn't stand the feeling of her hair restrained. She needed it loose, soft, falling where it wanted to fall.

In the bedroom, she opened her closet and considered the options. Everything inside was muted, earthy, gentle on the eye—sage linens, cream cashmere, dusty blues and soft grays. Clothes that draped rather than clung. Clothes that suggested a woman with nothing to prove.

She chose the cream linen pants, a dove-gray sweater that fell past her hips, soft wool socks in oatmeal. She never taught barefoot like Maya did. There was something too exposed about bare feet, too vulnerable. Mira preferred layers. Barriers. The soft armor of fabric between herself and the world.

At the small vanity in the corner of her bedroom, she opened her jewelry box. This was her one indulgence—rings and necklaces and earrings in silver and stone, collected over years of quiet accumulation. She slid three rings onto her fingers: a hammered silver band, an opal that caught the light, a thin gold snake that wound around her pinky. A long pendant around her neck—raw amethyst on a leather cord. Moonstone earrings that would sway when she moved.

Maya wore almost no jewelry. Just small gold studs and a delicate ankle bracelet that had become her signature. The students recognized it; they'd given her the bracelet as a gift years ago, and she never took it off.

Mira's jewelry was different. Heavier. More present. She liked the weight of it on her body, the way it announced her movements with small sounds and glints of light.

The final touch: she uncapped a small glass bottle and dabbed oil at her wrists and throat. Sandalwood and vetiver. Grounding. Earthy. The smell of quiet rooms and held breath.

Maya's scent was citrus and ginger—bright, sharp, impossible to ignore. Mira sometimes caught traces of it when they passed each other in the studio hallway, that bright burst of her sister's presence lingering in the air.

They were so different, the two of them. Had always been, even as children. Maya was fire and light and relentless forward motion. Mira was water and shadow and the patience of deep roots. Maya built things up; Mira kept them from falling down. It was a good system. It had always been a good system.

She gathered her things—a soft leather yoga bag, worn at the corners, so different from Maya's sleek black one—and left the apartment.

Mira always walked to the studio. Maya took cabs, always in a hurry, always running five minutes behind despite her best efforts. But Mira liked the rhythm of walking, the way the city changed texture as she moved through it. The anonymity of being just another woman on the sidewalk, unremarkable, unseen.

By the time she arrived, the sun had begun its slow descent into the gap between buildings. She climbed the stairs to the third floor—the smaller space, the one used for gentler practices—and began preparing the room.

Bolsters against the wall. Blankets in perfect thirds. Eye pillows lined up like sleeping birds. Salt lamps casting amber pools across the hardwood.

This was her favorite class to teach. Not Maya's power vinyasa sessions, all heat and sweat and triumphant exhaustion. Mira preferred this—the slow unwinding, the permission to be still. Yin yoga. Restorative. The practices that asked nothing except presence.

Students filtered in. A woman in her sixties with careful posture and sad eyes. A young man who looked like he hadn't slept in days. A pair of friends whispering as they claimed spots near the back. They moved quietly, reverently, as if entering a church.

In a way, they were.

"Welcome," Mira said once everyone had settled. Her voice was lower than Maya's, softer, with a quality one student had described as "like being wrapped in something warm." She'd taken that as the highest compliment. "Find a comfortable seat. Let your eyes close if that feels safe. And just begin to notice your breath."

She watched them sink into themselves. This was the moment she loved—the visible release, the shoulders dropping, the faces smoothing out. They came to her carrying so much. Jobs they hated. Relationships that were dying. Grief they couldn't name. They carried it in their bodies, in the tension of their jaws and the armor of their spines, and they didn't even know they were doing it.

She knew. She always knew.

"We hold so much," she continued, barely above a whisper. "We hold without realizing we're holding. Tonight, we practice letting go. Not forcing. Not pushing. Just... releasing what's ready to be released."

She guided them into the first pose—a supported child's pose, bolsters under their torsos, foreheads resting on stacked fists. Five minutes of stillness. Five minutes of breathing into the lower back, the hips, the places where fear liked to hide.

Mira moved through the room while they held. This was when she did her best work—the quiet adjustments, a hand on a shoulder here, a gentle press into a lower back there. Her rings caught the lamplight as she moved.

She paused beside the older woman with the sad eyes. Knelt down. Placed one hand between her shoulder blades and one at the base of her skull.

"Breathe here," she whispered. "Let me hold this for a moment."

The woman made a small sound—not quite a sob, not quite a sigh. Something between. Mira felt it move through her palm, all that compressed grief finally finding an exit.

"Good," Mira said. "That's good. Let it go."

She stayed there for a long moment, longer than she usually would. There was something about this woman. A particular quality of sorrow that felt almost familiar.

When she finally moved on, she noticed something on the floor near the woman's mat. A small gold earring, the backing missing, half-hidden under the edge of a blanket.

Mira picked it up. Held it in her palm.

The metal was still warm from the woman's body. Such a small thing. Such a small loss.

She should return it. Obviously. The woman had probably taken it off before class and forgotten. The right thing to do was tap her shoulder, hand it back, watch her face flood with relief.

Instead, Mira slipped it into her pocket.

She didn't know why. She never knew why, not really. It was just something she did. Had always done, as far back as she could remember. Small things. Things that wouldn't be missed, or at least not immediately. A hair tie left on a locker room bench. A tube of lip balm forgotten in a bathroom. A ring placed carefully by a sink.

She didn't wear them or sell them. She just kept them. In a

box in her closet that no one else knew about. Proof, maybe, that these people had been real. That they had trusted her with their bodies, their breath, their grief. That she had mattered to them, even if they didn't know her name the next day.

It wasn't stealing. Not really. They were offerings. Gifts left at the altar of her attention.

She moved on to the next student. And the next. By the end of the class, seventy-five minutes later, she had guided them through six poses, three meditations, and a yoga nidra that left half of them snoring softly on their mats.

"Take your time coming back," she said as she brought them out of the final relaxation. "There's no rush. There's nowhere else you need to be."

They stirred slowly, blinking like people emerging from a vivid dream. A few of them cried. This happened often in her classes—something about the stillness cracked people open in ways movement couldn't.

The older woman approached her as the room emptied.

"Thank you," she said. Her eyes were red-rimmed but somehow lighter. "I don't know what you did, but... thank you."

Mira took her hands. Held them. "You did the work. I just held space."

The woman nodded, squeezed Mira's fingers, and turned to go. She didn't notice the missing earring. She wouldn't, probably, until she got home. And by then she'd assume it had fallen off on the subway, or in her building lobby, or in any of the thousand places that weren't here.

Mira watched her leave. Then she began the ritual of closing —adjusting props, wiping mats, turning off the salt lamps one by one.

Her phone buzzed. Maya.

"Hey, it's me." Her sister's voice on the voicemail was tight, controlled, with something frantic underneath. "Call me when you get this. We need to talk."

Mira listened to the message twice. Then she deleted it.

She wasn't ready to talk to Maya. Not tonight. Maya would want to process the interview, to dissect every question and answer, to strategize about what came next. Maya always wanted to talk, to plan, to control.

Mira just wanted quiet.

She finished closing up and stepped into the night. The city was cooler now, the earlier urgency softened into something almost peaceful. She walked the fourteen blocks to her apartment rather than taking the subway. She liked walking at night. The anonymity of it, the way she could move through the world without being seen.

Her building was a brownstone on a tree-lined street—beautiful in a way that suggested money without screaming it. She climbed the stairs to the third floor, unlocked her door, and stepped into darkness.

She didn't turn on the lights. She never did, not right away. There was something she liked about moving through her own space by feel, by memory. Knowing exactly where every piece of furniture was. Knowing the exact number of steps from the door to the bedroom to the closet.

The closet.

She slid the door open and knelt down, pushing aside a row of hanging clothes to reveal a shelf built into the back wall. The shelf held two boxes.

The first was small, covered in worn velvet. She opened it and added tonight's earring to the collection inside. It clinked softly against the others—a silver ring, a gold bangle, a pendant in the shape of a feather, a watch with a cracked face. She didn't count them anymore. There were too many to count.

The second box was larger. Wooden. Brass latch.

She ran her fingers over the lid but didn't open it. Not tonight. Tonight she was tired.

She closed the closet door and moved to the bathroom, where she washed her face and brushed her teeth without turning on the light. The mirror was just a shape in the darkness, a rectangle of nothing.

That was fine. She didn't need to see herself tonight.

She crawled into bed and lay there for a long time, staring at the ceiling, thinking about the woman with the sad eyes. About the sound she'd made when Mira touched her. About all the pain people carried without knowing they were carrying it.

She thought about Maya's voicemail. The tightness in her sister's voice. Whatever had happened in that interview, it had rattled her.

Mira would deal with it tomorrow. She always dealt with things. That was her role—the one who handled, the one who fixed, the one who made problems disappear. Maya was the face. Mira was the hands.

She closed her eyes.

Just before sleep took her, she heard something. A voice, maybe. Or the memory of a voice. Small and frightened and very far away.

Why do you take things that aren't yours?

She didn't answer. She didn't need to.

Some questions were better left in the dark.

3

Celeste
The Assignment

The photograph lived in the bottom drawer of Celeste's desk, underneath a stack of old notebooks and a press pass from a job she no longer had.

She didn't look at it often. Looking at it served no purpose—didn't change anything, didn't bring anyone back, didn't answer any of the questions that had been eating at her for four years. But sometimes, late at night when the apartment was too quiet and her thoughts were too loud, she would slide open the drawer and hold the photograph in her hands and remember what it felt like to have a sister.

Bree smiled up at her from the glossy paper. Twenty-two years old, sun-brown and laughing, wearing a backpack that was almost comically overstuffed. The airport terminal stretched out behind her, blurred faces and rolling suitcases and departure screens announcing flights to everywhere.

Going to find myself, Bree had texted that morning, along with a string of emojis—prayer hands, a lotus flower, a little cartoon airplane. *Don't worry about me. I'll be back before you know it.*

That was the last normal message Celeste ever received from her.

She closed the drawer.

It was Tuesday morning, gray and spitting rain, and she had a pitch meeting in an hour that she wasn't remotely prepared for. The magazine—a mid-tier lifestyle publication called *Wellspring* that covered wellness trends for women with disposable income—had been hinting for weeks that they needed fresh ideas, new angles, content that would "drive engagement" and "build community" and all the other phrases that meant nothing and everything at once.

Celeste had been a journalist for eight years. She'd started at a scrappy digital outlet covering local politics, worked her way up to investigative features at a regional newspaper, and then watched that newspaper die the slow death that was claiming all newspapers everywhere. *Wellspring* was supposed to be temporary. A paycheck while she figured out her next move. That was three years ago.

Now she wrote articles with titles like "10 Adaptogens That Will Change Your Morning Routine" and "What Your Yoga Practice Says About Your Attachment Style." She interviewed influencers and wellness entrepreneurs and women who had built empires out of smoothie recipes and positive affirmations. She was, by all external metrics, successful. She had a byline. She had a salary. She had health insurance.

She had never felt more like a fraud in her life.

Her laptop pinged. An email from her editor, Rachel, with the subject line: *Pitch meeting pushed to 10:30. Also, I have an idea for you.*

Celeste typed back: *An idea or an assignment?*

The response came immediately: *Both. Come to my office when you get in.*

Twenty minutes later, Celeste was sitting across from Rachel's desk, nursing a coffee that had gone cold somewhere between the subway and the elevator. Rachel was one of those women who seemed to exist in a permanent state of polished competence—hair always blown out, nails always done, a closet full of blazers in every shade of beige. She was also, despite her corporate veneer, one of the sharper editors Celeste had worked with. She noticed things. She asked questions. She didn't accept the easy answer when a harder one was available.

It was the only reason Celeste had stayed this long.

"Prana and Bones," Rachel said, sliding a folder across the desk. "You know them?"

Celeste's stomach tightened. She kept her face neutral. "The yoga empire. Sisters who built it together. Ted Talk, supplement line, retreats with celebrity waitlists. Sure, I know them."

"Good. I want you to profile them." Rachel leaned back in her chair. "The angle is sisterhood. Partnership. How two women built something massive without killing each other. Feel-good stuff, but with depth. You know how to do depth."

Celeste opened the folder. Press clippings, headshots, a printout of the Prana & Bones website. Maya Sharma smiled up at her from a professional photograph—beautiful, serene, the kind of face that belonged on the cover of a magazine about inner peace.

"Why me?" Celeste asked. "This seems more like a Sarah piece."

"Sarah's on maternity leave. And honestly?" Rachel tilted her head. "I think you'll find something interesting. You always do. There's something about these two that feels... I don't know. Curated. Like the story they're telling isn't quite the whole story."

"You want me to dig."

"I want you to look. There's a difference." Rachel smiled. "You have a month. The cover slot for June is yours if you deliver something good."

Celeste looked at the photograph again. Maya Sharma's eyes were dark and warm and revealed absolutely nothing.

"I'll need access," she said. "Real access. Not just a publicist-approved interview in some meditation room."

"Get what you can. You're persuasive."

Celeste closed the folder and stood to leave. At the door, she paused.

"The sister," she said. "Mira. Has anyone actually met her?"

Rachel frowned. "What do you mean?"

"I mean—" Celeste hesitated. "I've been reading up on them. There are hundreds of photos of Maya. Interviews, videos, podcasts. But Mira is like a ghost. A few teaching shots, some quotes in articles, but nothing substantial. No interviews. No public appearances. For someone who supposedly runs half the business, she's remarkably invisible."

Rachel's frown deepened. "Maybe she's private."

"Maybe." Celeste tucked the folder under her arm. "Or maybe there's a reason she doesn't want to be seen."

She walked back to her desk, mind already churning. Prana & Bones. She'd known the name for years, of course—everyone in the wellness world did. But she'd avoided looking too closely. Avoided the website, the social media, the glowing profiles in publications just like this one.

Because Prana & Bones was where Bree had gone.

Four years ago, her little sister had scraped together her savings and flown to Mexico for a Prana & Bones retreat. A ten-day intensive in Tulum, promises of transformation and healing and finding your true self. Bree had been struggling—a bad breakup, a job she hated, the kind of existential crisis that hits some people in their early twenties and never quite lets go. The retreat was supposed to help. It was supposed to fix things.

Bree came back different.

Not bad different. Not obviously. She was calmer, she said. More centered. She'd had "breakthroughs" she couldn't fully explain. She'd met people who understood her in ways her family never had.

And then, slowly, she started to disappear.

First it was the phone calls that went unanswered. Then the family dinners she skipped. Then the apartment she gave up, the job she quit, the savings account she emptied to pay for more retreats, more trainings, more time in the orbit of Maya and Mira Sharma.

The last time Celeste saw her sister in person was two years ago. Bree had been thin—too thin—with a glassy look in her eyes and a vocabulary full of words like "surrender" and "ego death" and "the work." She'd told Celeste she was moving to an ashram. That she needed to "go deeper." That her family was "holding her back from her evolution."

"You don't understand," Bree had said. "You've never understood. Maya sees me. She really sees me."

Six months later, Bree stopped responding to messages entirely. Her phone was disconnected. Her email bounced back. The ashram—when Celeste finally tracked down its location—said that no one by that name had ever stayed there.

Bree was gone.

Not dead. Celeste didn't believe she was dead. But gone in a way that felt almost worse—erased, absorbed, dissolved into something Celeste couldn't name or fight or find.

And every trail, every thread, every unanswered question led back to the same place.

Prana & Bones.

Celeste sat down at her desk and opened the folder again.

She spread out the clippings, the photographs, the carefully constructed mythology of two sisters who had turned grief into gold.

Rachel thought she was assigning a puff piece. A feel-good profile about sisterhood and success.

She had no idea what she was actually unleashing.

Celeste pulled out her phone and began composing an email. Polite, professional, the kind of request a lifestyle journalist would send when she wanted access to a wellness empire.

Dear Ms. Sharma, she typed. *I'm working on a feature about the power of sibling partnerships in business, and I would love the opportunity to speak with you and your sister about your remarkable journey...*

The lies came easily. They always did when you needed them to.

She hit send.

Then she opened her bottom drawer, looked at Bree's smiling face one more time, and whispered: "I'm going to find out what happened to you. I promise."

The photograph didn't answer.

But somewhere, in a studio across the city, her email arrived in Maya Sharma's inbox.

And something that had been still for a very long time began, slowly, to wake up.

4

Maya
The Lie We Tell

The video had forty-seven million views.

Maya sat in her office—a small room behind the main studio, decorated with the same careful intentionality as everything else in the Prana & Bones empire—and watched herself on the screen. Three years ago, a different stage, a different woman. Or maybe the same woman, just better at hiding.

"I was twenty-three," the Maya on screen said. She stood in a pool of light, a red circle beneath her feet, speaking to an audience she couldn't see. Her voice was steady, warm, practiced. "I had just graduated. I had a job I thought I wanted, an apartment I thought I loved, and a boyfriend I thought would save me."

A pause. The audience waited.

"His name doesn't matter. What matters is what he taught me—not through love, but through control. Through isolation. Through the slow, systematic dismantling of everything I thought I knew about myself."

Maya watched her past self move across the stage. The

gestures were good—open palms, measured steps, the occasional press of hand to heart. She'd rehearsed for weeks. Had worked with a speaking coach who charged five hundred dollars an hour. Had practiced the pauses, the catches in her voice, the moments where she let her eyes shine with unshed tears.

"He told me I was too much. Too loud, too ambitious, too needy. He told me my friends were toxic, my family was holding me back, my dreams were unrealistic. And because I loved him—because I thought this was what love looked like—I believed him."

She'd told this story so many times now that it felt true. That was the strange thing about lies—tell them long enough and they started to grow roots. Started to feel like memories. Sometimes, late at night, Maya could almost picture him. The boyfriend who didn't exist. The apartment where she'd never lived. The slow suffocation of a relationship that had never happened.

"Yoga saved my life," the video Maya continued. "Not right away. Not dramatically. But breath by breath, pose by pose, I started to find my way back to myself. I started to remember that I was a person. That I had a right to take up space. That my voice mattered."

The audience applauded. Maya had known they would. That was the thing about stories like this—they were irresistible. Everyone wanted to believe that suffering had meaning, that pain could be alchemized into purpose, that the worst things that happened to you could become the foundation for the best things.

She paused the video.

The story wasn't hers. She'd stolen it.

Not intentionally. Not at first. It had started in a sharing circle during her very first yoga teacher training, fifteen years ago. A woman named Renata—dark-haired, soft-spoken, with bruises on her wrists she tried to hide with bracelets—had told the group about her ex-boyfriend. The control. The isolation. The slow erasure of self.

Maya had listened. Had felt something stir in her chest—not sympathy exactly, but recognition. Recognition of the power in that story. The way it made Renata untouchable, sacred, worthy of protection and praise.

Maya wanted that. She didn't have her own story of survival—not one she could tell, anyway. What had happened in her childhood, the thing with her father, the years that followed—none of that could be spoken aloud. None of that would make her sympathetic.

So she borrowed Renata's story. Just a few details at first, woven into conversations. Then more. Then all of it, reshaped and refined, the names changed and the timeline adjusted until it fit her perfectly.

By the time she gave the Ted Talk, Renata's story had become Maya's origin myth. The foundation of everything.

And Renata?

Renata had seen the video. Had reached out, once, through the website's contact form. A confused, hurt message asking why Maya was telling her story, her exact words, her private pain.

Mira had handled it. Mira always handled things.

Maya didn't know what her sister had said or done. She didn't ask. She just knew that Renata never contacted them again. That the message disappeared from the inbox. That the problem had been solved, the way all their problems were eventually solved.

She closed the laptop and pressed her fingers to her temples.

The interview this morning had unsettled her. The journalist—Celeste—had looked at her with those sharp, knowing eyes, and Maya had felt, for just a moment, like she was being seen. Not the version of herself she presented to the world, but something underneath. Something she kept hidden even from herself.

That story means a lot to people, Celeste had said. *It meant a lot to someone I know.*

What did that mean? Who did she know?

Maya's phone rang. She looked at the screen, expecting Mira, hoping for Mira.

It was her mother.

She let it go to voicemail. She always let it go to voicemail. Sunita Sharma called once a month, like clockwork, and once a month Maya ignored her. It had been almost two years since they'd spoken—really spoken, not just Maya declining calls and deleting voicemails without listening to them.

She couldn't even remember exactly what had caused the rift. A fight about something. A conversation that had gone wrong. Her mother had been upset, saying things that didn't make sense, and Maya had hung up and told herself she'd call back when things calmed down.

She never did.

It wasn't that she hated her mother. She didn't. She just couldn't handle the weight of Sunita's worry, the endless questions, the way every conversation felt like an interrogation disguised as concern. *Are you sleeping? Are you eating? Are you taking care of yourself? You work too hard. You push too hard. I'm worried about you, beta.*

It was easier to let Mira handle it. Mira had always been better with their mother anyway—more patient, more willing to sit through the long silences and the circular conversations. Let Mira be the good daughter. Maya had an empire to run.

She shook her head and picked up her phone to call her

sister. She needed Mira's voice, steady and calm, telling her that everything was fine. That the journalist was nobody. That there was nothing to worry about.

She dialed. It rang once, twice, three times.

"Hey." Mira's voice on the other end. "I got your message. What's wrong?"

Maya felt her whole body relax. "The interview. It was weird. The journalist was asking questions—about you, about us, about why there aren't photos of us together."

A pause. "What did you tell her?"

"The usual. That you hate cameras. That you're private."

"Good."

"But Mira, she knew something. I could feel it. She asked about the Ted Talk. About my story. She said it meant a lot to someone she knew."

Another pause, longer this time. "Did she say who?"

"No. But the way she looked at me—" Maya pressed her free hand against her chest, where the anxiety was building like pressure in a sealed container. "I don't like it. Something's off."

"Okay." Mira's voice was calm, controlled. The voice she used when she was thinking. "I'll look into her. Find out who she is, what she's really after."

"How? How will you look into her?"

"I have ways. You know that."

Maya did know. She'd never asked about Mira's ways, and Mira had never offered details. There was an understanding between them, unspoken but absolute: Maya was the light, and Mira was the shadow. Maya built things up, and Mira cleared the path. Whatever that required.

"Will you come over tonight?" Maya asked. "I could make dinner. Open some wine. I feel like I haven't seen you in forever."

A brief hesitation. Then: "Sure. I'll come by around eight."

"Really?" Maya couldn't hide her surprise. Mira usually declined these invitations—she preferred her own space, her own rhythms, her solitude. "That would be... I would love that. I'll make that pasta you like. The one with the lemon and the capers."

"Sounds perfect." Warmth in Mira's voice now. "I'll see you tonight. And Maya?"

"Yeah?"

"Stop worrying. Everything is going to be fine. I promise."

"I know. I just—"

"I know. That's why I'm coming over. We'll figure it out together. Like we always do."

"I love you," Maya said.

"I love you too." The line went dead.

Maya sat for a long moment in the silence of her office. She felt better already. Tonight they would eat pasta and drink wine and talk through the situation like they always did. Mira would have ideas. Mira always had ideas.

She stood up and stretched. She had a class to teach at noon, and then she needed to stop by the market for lemons and capers and a good bottle of white wine. She wanted everything to be perfect.

It had been too long since they'd had an evening like this. Just the two of them, the way it used to be.

She walked out of her office and into the bright, clean space of the studio.

"Welcome," she said to the arriving students. "Let's begin."

5

Mira
Sisters

Maya spent the afternoon preparing.

She left the studio at three, stopping at the Italian market on the corner for fresh pasta and a wedge of parmesan and lemons so yellow they looked painted. She bought capers packed in salt, the good kind, and a bottle of Sancerre that the shop owner recommended with a knowing smile. She bought candles—unnecessary, probably, but she wanted the apartment to feel warm. Welcoming.

It had been months since Mira had come over. Maybe longer. They talked every day, of course, but Mira preferred her own space. She was like a cat that way—affectionate on her own terms, easily overwhelmed by too much togetherness. Maya had learned long ago not to push. To appreciate the closeness they had without demanding more.

But tonight, Mira was coming. Tonight they would sit across from each other at Maya's small kitchen table and drink wine and talk like they used to.

Maya showered and changed into soft clothes—cashmere

sweater, worn jeans, bare feet. She pulled her hair up into its usual ponytail, then hesitated, looking at herself in the mirror. Should she leave it down? Mira always wore her hair down. Maybe—

No. She was being ridiculous. This was Mira. Her sister. She didn't need to be anyone other than herself.

She started the pasta water at 7:45. Opened the wine to let it breathe. Lit the candles on the table and dimmed the overhead lights until the apartment glowed amber and gold.

At 8:02, she heard the key in the lock.

"It's me," Mira called out.

"In the kitchen!"

Maya heard the door close, heard footsteps crossing the living room, and then her sister appeared in the kitchen doorway.

Mira looked the way she always looked—soft where Maya was sharp, contained where Maya was expansive. Her dark hair fell loose around her shoulders, and she wore a cream-colored sweater that looked like it had been washed a hundred times. Silver rings glinted on her fingers. She smelled like sandalwood.

"You look nice," Mira said.

"So do you." Maya handed her a glass of wine. "I'm so glad you came."

"Me too." Mira took a sip, watching Maya over the rim of the glass. "You seemed rattled on the phone. That's not like you."

"I know. It's stupid. The interview just got under my skin." Maya turned back to the stove, dropping pasta into the boiling water. "There was something about that woman. Celeste. Like she was looking for something specific."

"She's a journalist. They always look like that. It's how they make you say more than you meant to."

"Maybe." Maya stirred the pasta. "Did you find anything? About her?"

"Some." Mira settled onto one of the kitchen stools. "She's been at *Wellspring* for about three years. Before that, newspaper work. Nothing remarkable."

"So why does she feel remarkable?"

"I'm still looking into it." Mira's voice was carefully neutral. "There might be a personal connection. Someone she knows who's encountered us before."

"Encountered us? What does that mean?"

"It means I'm still figuring it out. But I will. I always do."

They worked in comfortable silence for a few minutes—Maya finishing the pasta, Mira watching from her perch at the counter. The kitchen filled with the smell of lemon and butter and good wine.

"Mom called today," Maya said finally, not looking up from the stove.

"I know. She told me."

Maya turned. "You talked to her?"

"I talk to her every week." Mira said it simply, without judgment, but something in her tone made Maya's chest tighten. "You know that."

"I know. I just..." Maya shook her head, turning back to the pasta. "I don't know how you do it. Every conversation with her feels like she's trying to dig something out of me."

"She's worried about you. That's all it is."

"She's always worried. She's been worried my whole life. It's exhausting."

"She's our mother, Maya. That's what mothers do."

Maya plated the pasta in silence, carrying the bowls to the small table by the window. The city glittered below them, indifferent to the conversation happening three stories above.

"What does she say?" Maya asked, sitting down across from her sister. "When you talk to her?"

"She asks about the business. About how you're doing. Whether you're sleeping, eating, taking care of yourself." Mira twirled pasta around her fork. "She asks about me too, but mostly she wants to know about you."

"And what do you tell her?"

"That you're fine. That we're both fine. That she doesn't need to worry."

"Is that true?"

Mira looked up, her dark eyes unreadable in the candlelight. "Is what true?"

"That I'm fine."

A pause. Then Mira smiled—small, private, the smile she saved for moments when Maya was being particularly transparent. "You're always fine, Maya. You don't know how to be anything else."

"That's not an answer."

"It's the only answer I have."

They ate in silence for a while. The pasta was good—bright with lemon, salty with capers, rich with butter and parmesan. Outside, the city hummed its endless hum.

"She wants to see you," Mira said finally. "Mom. She asked me to tell you."

"I know."

"She's getting older, Maya. She won't be here forever."

"I know that too."

"Then why won't you call her back?"

Maya set down her fork. "It's complicated."

"It's not, actually. She's your mother. She loves you. She wants to hear your voice. That's not complicated at all."

"You don't understand."

"Then explain it to me."

But Maya couldn't explain it. Couldn't put into words the way her mother's voice made her feel—small, scrutinized, somehow wrong. The way every conversation felt like a test she was failing. The way Sunita looked at her sometimes, with an expression Maya couldn't read, as if she were searching for someone else behind Maya's eyes.

"I'll call her," Maya said finally. "Soon. I promise."

"You always say that."

"I mean it this time."

Mira didn't argue. She just nodded and returned to her pasta, and Maya was grateful for the silence.

After dinner, they moved to the couch with what was left of the wine. Maya tucked her feet underneath her and leaned into the cushions. Mira sat at the other end, her posture perfect as always.

"I should go soon," Mira said. "Early morning tomorrow."

"Already?" Maya glanced at the clock. It was barely ten. "Stay a little longer."

"You know I don't like to be out late."

"I know. But I like having you here." Maya heard the neediness in her own voice and hated it. "I'm sorry. I'm being clingy."

"You're being human." Mira stood, collecting her bag. "But I really do need to go."

Maya walked her to the door. They stood for a moment in the entryway, facing each other.

"Thank you for coming," Maya said. "And for... you know. Talking to Mom. Keeping that connection alive when I can't."

"Someone has to." But there was no accusation in Mira's voice. Just fact.

"Tell her I love her? Next time you talk?"

"Tell her yourself."

Maya smiled despite herself. "You're relentless."

"That's why you keep me around." Mira leaned in and

pressed a kiss to Maya's forehead—quick, almost perfunctory, but tender. "Lock the door behind me. And stop worrying."

"Promise?"

"Promise."

Maya watched her sister walk down the hallway toward the elevator. Watched until she rounded the corner and disappeared. Then she closed the door, turned the lock, and stood for a long moment in the sudden silence.

The apartment felt emptier now. Colder, despite the candles still flickering on the table.

She should call her mother. Mira was right—Sunita wouldn't be here forever. Whatever had happened between them, whatever strange tension had driven them apart, it wasn't worth losing her entirely.

Tomorrow, Maya told herself. She would call tomorrow.

She blew out the candles and carried the dishes to the sink.

Tomorrow. She would definitely call tomorrow.

6

Celeste
The Inconsistencies

The fluorescent lights in the *Wellspring* office hummed at a frequency that Celeste was convinced had been specifically engineered to cause migraines.

She sat at her desk—a narrow rectangle in the open-plan bullpen, wedged between a woman who wrote about crystals and a man who specialized in "plant-based masculinity," whatever that meant—and stared at the notes spread out before her. Three days since the interview with Maya Sharma. Three days of digging, and the more she dug, the less anything made sense.

She'd started with the basics. Prana & Bones had been founded twelve years ago, starting as a single studio in a converted warehouse in Queens. From there, it had grown into something approaching an empire: four studios across three cities, a teacher training program with a two-year waitlist, a supplement line sold in Whole Foods, an annual retreat in Tulum that cost more than some people's monthly rent.

At the center of it all: two sisters. Maya, the face. Mira, the heart.

Celeste had heard Maya say that exact phrase in at least six different interviews. It was good branding—the yin and yang of sisterhood, complementary opposites building something neither could have built alone. The wellness industry loved that kind of narrative. It suggested balance, wholeness, the integration of shadow and light.

But when Celeste tried to trace the details, the narrative started to blur.

She'd pulled every interview she could find with Maya Sharma. There were dozens—podcasts, magazine profiles, video segments on morning shows. Maya was polished and consistent, hitting the same beats every time: the father's death, the discovery of yoga, the years of building, the partnership with her sister.

Mira, by contrast, was almost invisible.

Celeste had found exactly three interviews with Mira Sharma. One was a brief quote in a trade publication about the supplement line. One was a short video clip from a teacher training, where Mira demonstrated a restorative pose while speaking softly about the importance of surrender. The third was an email interview—written responses to written questions—for a small yoga blog that had since gone defunct.

No podcasts. No video profiles. No appearances alongside her sister at industry events or award ceremonies. For someone who supposedly ran half of a multimillion-dollar business, Mira Sharma was remarkably, almost aggressively, absent from the public record.

She's private, Maya had said. *She hates cameras.*

Maybe. Some people were genuinely camera-shy. But this felt like something more than shyness. This felt like strategy.

Celeste pulled up the Prana & Bones website and clicked through the photo galleries. Classes, retreats, teacher trainings, community events. Hundreds of images spanning more than a decade.

Maya appeared in at least half of them. Teaching, smiling, hugging students, accepting awards. Her face was everywhere—radiant, present, impossible to miss.

Mira appeared in maybe a dozen. Always at a distance, always partially obscured—her face turned away from the camera, or hidden behind another person, or blurred as if she'd moved at the moment of capture. In several photos, only a sliver of her was visible: a shoulder, a hand, the edge of her distinctive silver jewelry.

And in not a single image—not one, out of hundreds—were Maya and Mira photographed together.

Celeste leaned back in her chair, chewing on the end of her pen.

Sisters who had built an empire together. Sisters who, by Maya's own account, had "never spent more than a week apart" in their adult lives. Sisters who apparently couldn't manage to stand next to each other for a single photograph.

It was possible, she supposed. Some families were just like that—private, compartmentalized, more comfortable in parallel than in proximity. But Celeste had spent enough years as a journalist to know when something didn't add up. And this didn't add up.

She opened a new browser tab and typed in *Mira Sharma yoga teacher*.

The results were sparse. A few mentions in articles about Prana & Bones, always in connection to Maya. A sparse Instagram account—@mira.sharma.yoga—with fewer than a thousand followers and posts that appeared every few weeks: images of nature, quotes about stillness, the occasional glimpse of hands in meditation or feet on a yoga mat. No face. Never a face.

Celeste clicked through the followers list, looking for patterns. Students, mostly. A few other yoga teachers. Some wellness brands. Nothing that suggested close personal relationships, friendships, a life outside the studio walls.

She tried a different search: *Maya Sharma sister* and *Sharma family yoga*.

More of the same. The origin story repeated across multiple outlets, always in Maya's voice. Their father had died when they were young—a hiking accident, tragic and sudden. Their mother had taken them to a grief counselor who incorporated yoga. From that loss, a calling had emerged.

But where were the childhood photos? The old friends who remembered them? The teachers who had trained them, the mentors who had guided them? Every successful person left a trail of relationships behind them—people who could vouch for their history, confirm their story, fill in the gaps.

Maya and Mira Sharma seemed to have sprung fully formed from the head of Zeus, with no past and no connections beyond the empire they'd built.

Celeste's phone buzzed. A text from her mother: *Thinking about you. Dinner Sunday?*

She ignored it. She couldn't handle her mother right now—the gentle questions, the careful concern, the way every conversation eventually circled back to Bree.

Bree.

Celeste closed her eyes and saw her sister's face. The last time, two years ago. Too thin, too bright, talking too fast about things Celeste couldn't follow.

You don't understand. You've never understood. Maya sees me. She really sees me.

Maya. Not *they*. Not *Maya and Mira*. Just Maya.

At the time, Celeste hadn't noticed the distinction. But now, replaying the conversation in her memory, she wondered. Had

Bree ever mentioned Mira? Had she ever spoken about the other sister, the quiet one, the one who handled things behind the scenes?

She couldn't remember. The whole conversation had been so strange, so disconnected from the sister she'd grown up with, that Celeste had spent most of it just trying to keep up. Trying to find the Bree she knew underneath all the new vocabulary, the new certainties, the new walls.

She hadn't found her. And three months later, Bree had stopped responding entirely.

Celeste opened her eyes and looked at her notes again.

She needed more. More than Google searches and Instagram archaeology. She needed to talk to people who had actually been inside Prana & Bones. Students, staff, former employees. People who might have seen something, noticed something, wondered about the same inconsistencies that were keeping Celeste up at night.

She pulled up LinkedIn and started searching.

Former employees of Prana & Bones were easy enough to find. The company had grown fast, which meant turnover—people who had joined when it was small and left when it got big, people who had been pushed out or burned out or simply moved on. Celeste made a list of names, cross-referencing with public profiles, looking for anyone who might be willing to talk.

One name caught her attention: Jonah Whitfield. According to his LinkedIn, he'd worked as a senior teacher at Prana & Bones for three years before leaving abruptly. His current job was listed as "Fitness Instructor" at a chain gym in New Jersey —a significant step down from teaching at one of the most prestigious yoga studios in the city.

Celeste found his email through some creative searching and composed a message:

Dear Mr. Whitfield,

I'm a journalist working on a profile of Prana & Bones for Wellspring magazine. I'm reaching out to former employees to get a fuller picture of the organization. I'd love to hear about your experience there, on or off the record—whatever you're comfortable with.

Would you be open to a brief conversation?

Best, Celeste Park

She sent similar messages to four other names on her list, then sat back and waited.

It didn't take long. Within an hour, she had three polite declines, one non-response, and one reply that made her heart beat faster.

Jonah Whitfield had written back.

I'll talk to you. But not over email and not at my work. There's a coffee shop in Hoboken called The Grind. Meet me there tomorrow at 2pm. Come alone.

And Ms. Park? Be careful who else you contact about this. Some of these people are still loyal. And loyalty at Prana & Bones means something different than you might think.

Celeste read the message three times.

Then she marked the date in her calendar and started preparing her questions.

The Grind was exactly what the name suggested—a small, aggressively hip coffee shop with exposed brick, reclaimed wood tables, and a menu full of drinks that required a PhD to decode. Celeste arrived fifteen minutes early and claimed a table in the back corner where she could watch the door.

Jonah Whitfield walked in at 2:03. She recognized him from his LinkedIn photo, though he looked older in person—late thirties, with the kind of lean build that suggested he still worked out regularly, but tired around the eyes. He wore jeans and a hoodie and looked around the coffee shop with the wariness of a man who expected to be watched.

She raised her hand. He nodded and made his way over.

"Ms. Park?"

"Celeste, please." She gestured to the chair across from her. "Thank you for meeting me."

He sat down but didn't relax. His eyes kept flicking to the door, to the other customers, to the windows. "I almost didn't come."

"What changed your mind?"

"Curiosity, mostly." He flagged down a server and ordered a black coffee, nothing fancy. "And the fact that you're not the first person to come asking questions about Prana & Bones."

Celeste felt her pulse quicken. "Who else has asked?"

"A few people over the years. A reporter from some wellness blog. A woman who said her daughter had gotten 'too involved' with the organization. A private investigator, once, though he wouldn't say who hired him." Jonah shrugged. "They all went away eventually. Stopped calling, stopped emailing. Moved on to other things."

"What do you think happened to them?"

"I don't know. But I know what happened to me, and that's enough to make me paranoid."

The server brought his coffee. Jonah wrapped his hands around the mug but didn't drink.

"I worked at Prana & Bones for three years," he said. "Started as a regular teacher, worked my way up to senior instructor. I was good—really good. I had a following. Students requested me by name. I thought I was going to be there forever."

"What changed?"

"I started noticing things." He finally took a sip of his coffee. "Little things, at first. The way Maya sometimes didn't recognize me, even though we'd worked together for years. The way she'd call me by the wrong name, or reference conversations we'd never had. I thought she was just stressed, overworked. Running an empire takes a toll."

"But?"

"But then I started paying closer attention. And I realized it wasn't just forgetfulness. It was like... like she was a different person sometimes. The same face, the same voice, but something underneath had shifted. Her whole energy would change."

Celeste leaned forward. "Can you give me an example?"

Jonah set down his mug. "There was this one day—I'll never forget it. I was teaching a class, and Maya walked in to observe. She sat in the back, just watching. And afterward, she came up to me and said, 'That was beautiful, Jonah. You have such a gift for this work.' She was warm, present, completely Maya."

He paused.

"Then, maybe two hours later, I ran into her in the hallway. I said something like, 'Thanks again for the kind words,' and she looked at me like I was speaking a foreign language. 'What words?' she asked. And when I reminded her, she got this strange look on her face and said, 'That wasn't me. That must have been Mira.'"

Celeste felt a chill run down her spine. "She said it was Mira who observed your class?"

"That's what she said. But here's the thing." Jonah lowered his voice. "I've worked at that studio for three years. I've seen Maya hundreds of times. I've seen Mira teach—she does the evening yin classes, keeps to herself, very different vibe. But in three years of working there, I never once saw them in the same room together. Not once."

"That could just be scheduling—"

"It's not scheduling." Jonah's voice was firm. "I paid attention after that conversation. Started tracking when Maya was around, when Mira was around. Their schedules were always opposite. When Maya was teaching, Mira was supposedly in a meeting, or traveling, or working from home. When Mira was in the studio, Maya was at a speaking engagement or a retreat."

"Did you ever ask anyone about it?"

"Once. I asked one of the other senior teachers if she'd ever seen them together. She got this weird look on her face and said, 'They're very private about their relationship. It's best not to ask.'"

"And then what happened?"

Jonah laughed, but there was no humor in it. "Then I made the mistake of asking Maya directly. I tried to be casual about it—said something like, 'I'd love to meet with you and your sister sometime, I've got some ideas to bounce off you both.' And Maya just smiled and said, 'Mira doesn't do meetings. She prefers to work alone.'"

"That doesn't sound—"

"A week later, I was accused of inappropriate conduct with a student."

Celeste went still. "What?"

"Three anonymous complaints, filed with the Yoga Alliance. Inappropriate adjustments during class. Making students uncomfortable. Sexual undertones." Jonah's jaw tightened. "I didn't do any of it. I've never touched a student in any way that wasn't completely professional. But it didn't matter. The accusations were enough. My certification was suspended pending investigation. Prana & Bones let me go immediately—'protecting the integrity of the community,' they said."

"Did you fight it?"

"I tried. But the complaints were anonymous. The Yoga Alliance wouldn't tell me who had filed them, wouldn't give me any details. And when I tried to talk to my former colleagues, to find students who could vouch for me, nobody wanted to get involved. They were scared."

"Scared of what?"

"Of ending up like me." Jonah finished his coffee and set the mug down with a thunk. "I lost everything, Ms. Park. My career, my reputation, my community. I spent two years trying to rebuild, and the best I could do was a job at a chain gym teaching spin classes to people who don't know my name."

"And you think Prana & Bones was behind the accusations?"

"I think someone at Prana & Bones was behind them. Someone who didn't like that I was asking questions. Someone who wanted me gone." He met her eyes. "I think the accusations were fabricated. All three of them. And I think whoever filed them knew exactly what they were doing."

Celeste thought about Mira. About the woman who handled things.

"Mr. Whitfield—"

"Jonah."

"Jonah. You said you never saw Maya and Mira together. But you did see them separately. What were the differences? How could you tell which one you were talking to?"

Jonah considered the question. "It was subtle. They look identical—same face, same features. But Maya always had her hair up, wore bright colors, moved like she owned every room she walked into. Mira wore her hair down, dressed in soft colors, moved more quietly. She had all these rings on her fingers—you could hear her coming sometimes, just from the sound of the jewelry."

"And their behavior?"

"Maya was warm. Charismatic. She made you feel like you were the only person in the room. Mira was... harder to read. Not unfriendly, but more contained. Like she was always watching, always calculating. Maya made you want to open up. Mira made you want to be careful."

"Did you ever feel like you were talking to the same person?"

Jonah was quiet for a long moment.

"Once," he said finally. "Just once. It was late—after nine PM. I'd stayed to finish some prep work for the next day. I thought I was alone in the studio, but then I heard footsteps. I came out of the back room and saw someone standing at the windows, looking out at the city."

"Maya or Mira?"

"That's just it—I couldn't tell. She was wearing all black, which neither of them usually did. Her hair was pulled back, but loosely, like it couldn't decide what it wanted to be. And when she turned and looked at me..."

He trailed off.

"What?" Celeste pressed.

"Her face was wrong. Not wrong like disfigured—wrong like blank. Like there was nobody behind the eyes. Like whoever usually lived in that body had stepped out for a moment, and the thing looking at me was just... waiting."

"What did you do?"

"I said something like, 'Sorry, I didn't know anyone was still here.' And she just stared at me for a long moment. Then she smiled—this perfect, beautiful smile that didn't reach her eyes—and said, 'There's always someone here, Jonah. That's what you don't understand.'"

"And then?"

"And then she walked past me and out the door. And when I got to the window and looked down at the street, she was gone. Like she'd never been there at all."

Celeste sat back in her chair, processing.

"I know how it sounds," Jonah said. "Crazy. Paranoid. But

I'm telling you what I saw. What I experienced. Something is wrong at Prana & Bones. Something with Maya, or Mira, or whoever she really is. And if you're planning to dig deeper, you need to understand what you're getting into."

"What do you think I'm getting into?"

Jonah stood up and dropped a few bills on the table for his coffee.

"I think there aren't two of them," he said quietly. "I don't think there ever were. I think Maya and Mira are the same person. And I think that person is very, very good at making problems disappear."

He walked out of the coffee shop without looking back.

Celeste sat alone at the table, her mind racing, her coffee growing cold beside her.

She had come looking for information about her sister. About what had happened to Bree, about why she had vanished into the orbit of Prana & Bones and never come back.

But now she was starting to wonder if the question wasn't *what had happened to Bree*.

The question was *who had happened to her*.

And whether the same thing was about to happen to Celeste.

7

Maya
The Gap

Maya woke up on the bathroom floor.

She didn't remember going to sleep there. She didn't remember going to sleep at all. The last thing she recalled with any clarity was standing at the kitchen sink after Mira left, washing the pasta pot, thinking about her mother and whether she should call.

Now it was—she squinted at the window, trying to gauge the light—morning? Early morning? The sky was that gray-pink color that could mean dawn or dusk, and her body couldn't tell which.

She pushed herself up slowly, every muscle aching like she'd run a marathon. The tile was cold against her palms. Her head throbbed.

She looked down at herself.

Fitted black leggings. A crimson tank top that showed her shoulders. Her gold ankle bracelet catching the dim light.

These were her clothes. Her favorite teaching outfit, actually

—the one she wore for the power vinyasa classes, the one that made her feel strong and commanding.

But she didn't remember putting them on.

The last thing she'd been wearing was the soft cashmere sweater and worn jeans from dinner with Mira. She'd been barefoot, relaxed, ready for bed. Now she was dressed for the studio, as if she'd been about to teach—or had just finished teaching.

How long had she been here?

She reached for her phone, which was somehow in the waistband of her leggings—an odd place to keep it—and checked the screen. 6:47 AM. Thursday.

Thursday.

The pasta dinner with Mira had been Tuesday night.

Maya stared at the phone, waiting for the numbers to rearrange themselves into something that made sense. They didn't. It was Thursday. She had lost Wednesday entirely.

A cold dread spread through her chest. She gripped the edge of the bathroom counter and pulled herself to standing, forcing herself to look in the mirror.

The face that stared back was hers. Same dark eyes, same cheekbones, same full mouth. She was still wearing makeup—more than she usually wore. Defined brows, bronzer, a tinted lip that had smeared slightly, probably from sleeping on the tile floor.

But that wasn't what made her freeze.

Her hair was down.

Loose around her shoulders, falling in soft waves. The way Mira wore her hair—always down, always soft, always taking up space in that gentle, uncontrolled way that Maya couldn't stand.

Maya never wore her hair down. Never. It was one of her rules, as fundamental as breathing. Hair up, always. Sleek, controlled, professional. That was who she was. That was who she had always been.

She tried to remember pulling it down. Tried to remember taking out the ponytail that she must have been wearing—because why else would she be dressed for teaching, in her power vinyasa clothes, if not to teach? She would have had her hair up. She always had her hair up when she taught.

But somewhere between teaching and ending up on the bathroom floor, her hair had come down. Had been let down. Had been styled into these soft waves that looked nothing like her and everything like—

Mira.

Maya's hands flew to her hair, yanking it back from her face, twisting it into a knot at the back of her head. Her fingers found a hair tie on her wrist—she didn't remember putting it there—and she wrapped it tight, too tight, pulling until her scalp ached.

Better. That was better.

But her hands were shaking now, and when she looked at herself in the mirror again—hair up, teaching clothes, smeared makeup—she saw a woman she didn't recognize.

Who had she been yesterday?

What had she done?

She pulled up her calendar with trembling fingers. Wednesday's schedule appeared on the screen:

7:00 AM — Morning meditation (personal) 9:00 AM — Staff meeting 12:00 PM — Power vinyasa (teach) 3:00 PM — Interview prep with publicist 6:00 PM — Private session with donor (Greenwell Foundation)

Five appointments. A full day of work. And Maya had no memory of any of it.

She scrolled to her text messages, looking for clues. There were several from yesterday that she didn't remember sending:

To Studio Manager, 8:52 AM: Running a few minutes late. Start without me.

To Publicist, 2:47 PM: Confirmed for 3. See you then.

To Mira, 5:15 PM: Greenwell session went well. Call me later?

The messages were in her voice, her cadence, her usual abbreviations. But she had no memory of typing them. No memory of the staff meeting or the class or the interview prep or the donor session. Nothing but a black void where Wednesday should have been.

A void during which she had apparently dressed for work, done her makeup, taught a class, conducted meetings, charmed a donor—and then come home, let her hair down like Mira always did, and collapsed on the bathroom floor.

Why the hair?

That was what she couldn't understand. The clothes made sense—she'd been working. The makeup made sense—she always wore makeup when she taught. But the hair. Why had she taken her hair down before passing out on the floor? Why had she styled it in those soft waves that she never wore, that she didn't even know how to create?

Unless she hadn't done it herself.

Unless someone else had been here. Unless someone else had found her and—

But that made no sense either. Who would come into her apartment and let her hair down? Who would style it into Mira's waves and then leave her unconscious on the bathroom tile?

Mira.

The thought came unbidden, unwanted.

What if Mira had come back? What if she had found Maya somehow incapacitated and had tried to help, and in the process had—

Had what? Styled her hair? That was absurd. That was the kind of thing a crazy person would think.

Maya pressed her palms against the cold counter and forced herself to breathe.

She was not crazy. She was stressed, overworked, losing time the way people sometimes did when they had too much on their plates. The hair was a fluke—maybe she'd taken it down before going to the bathroom and then passed out before she could get to bed. Maybe the waves were just what happened when her hair dried without being styled. Maybe she was making something out of nothing.

Her phone buzzed. A text from the studio manager: *Great class yesterday! Students are still raving. One of your best.*

Maya looked at the message. Looked at her reflection—hair now up, face pale beneath the smeared makeup, eyes wild with a fear she couldn't name.

She had taught a class. People had seen her. People were raving.

And she remembered none of it.

She turned on the shower and stepped under the water, still wearing her teaching clothes. The cold hit her like a slap, shocking her back into her body. She gasped, shuddered, forced herself to stay under the spray until her skin went numb and her teeth chattered and she felt, finally, present. Here. Real.

She peeled off the wet clothes and let them fall in a heap at her feet. Turned the water hot, then hotter, until the bathroom filled with steam and her skin flushed red. She washed her hair twice, scrubbing at her scalp like she could scour the missing hours from her mind.

When she finally stepped out, wrapped in a towel, she felt almost human again. Fragile, but functional. Whatever had happened yesterday, whatever gap had opened in her consciousness, she could deal with it later. Right now, she had a studio to run.

She dried her hair and pulled it back into its usual ponytail, tight and controlled. Applied fresh makeup with careful precision, hiding the dark circles, the pallor, the evidence of a night spent unconscious on the bathroom floor. Chose new clothes—different black leggings, a deep purple tank top, her usual gold studs.

She left the crimson tank top and the wet leggings in a pile on the bathroom floor. She couldn't look at them. Couldn't think about what they meant.

By the time she left the apartment, she looked like Maya Sharma, founder of Prana & Bones, wellness entrepreneur, woman who had it all together.

She didn't feel like that woman. She felt like something wearing that woman's skin.

But maybe that was enough. Maybe it had always been enough.

The studio was busy when she arrived. Thursday mornings always were—something about the approaching weekend made people want to sweat out their week, prepare their bodies for rest. Maya moved through the space with practiced ease, greeting students, adjusting props, radiating the calm confidence that was her trademark.

No one seemed to notice anything wrong. No one looked at her with concern or confusion. Whatever she had done yesterday, whoever she had been, had apparently passed for normal.

She checked in with the studio manager, a competent woman named Devi who had been with them for five years.

"Yesterday's class was incredible," Devi said, beaming. "I

peeked in for a few minutes. The energy was amazing. You seemed really... I don't know. Present. More than usual, even."

"Thanks." Maya forced a smile. "I was feeling inspired."

"The Greenwell donor was happy too. She already emailed asking about a monthly sponsorship arrangement. Said you really understood what she was looking for."

"That's great news."

"And your publicist called this morning—said the prep session was really productive, that you gave her some great new angles for the upcoming press push."

Maya nodded along, making the appropriate sounds, while inside, the void yawned wider.

She had done all of these things. Students had seen her, talked to her, taken class with her. And she remembered none of it.

After the morning rush settled, she retreated to her office and closed the door. Her hands were trembling again. She pressed them flat against the desk and focused on her breathing, the way she taught her students to do. In through the nose. Out through the mouth. Stay present. Stay here.

Her phone rang. Mira.

Maya grabbed it like a lifeline.

"Hey," she said, and her voice came out steadier than she felt. "I was just going to call you."

"I got your text last night," Mira said. "About the Greenwell session. Glad it went well."

"Yeah, it was..." Maya hesitated. "Mira, I need to ask you something."

"What's wrong? You sound strange."

"Did we talk yesterday? Other than that text?"

A pause. "No. I was busy all day. Why?"

"I just—" Maya pressed her free hand against her forehead. "I'm having trouble remembering yesterday. I woke up this morning and it's like... it's like the whole day is gone. I don't remember any of it."

Silence on the other end of the line.

"Mira?"

"That happens sometimes." Mira's voice was careful, neutral. "When you're stressed. You know that."

"Not like this. Not a whole day. I taught a class, I had meetings, I apparently charmed a donor into a monthly sponsorship, and I don't remember any of it."

"But you did those things. People saw you do them."

"That's what scares me." Maya's voice dropped to a whisper. "If I wasn't me yesterday, then who was I?"

Another pause. Longer this time.

"Maya," Mira said finally. "Listen to me. You're tired. You've been under a lot of stress with this journalist situation. Sometimes the mind protects itself by... stepping back for a while. Letting the body do what needs to be done without all the noise of conscious thought."

"That doesn't make sense."

"It makes perfect sense. It's dissociation. It's a trauma response. It's not dangerous—it's your brain taking care of you." Mira's voice was soothing, the voice she used in yoga nidra, the voice that made people feel safe. "Have you eaten today? Had any water?"

"No, I just—" Maya's voice cracked. "I woke up on the bathroom floor, Mira. In my teaching clothes. With my hair down. My hair was *down*, like—like how you wear yours. I never wear my hair down. Why would I—"

"You probably just took it down before bed and then got disoriented. It's nothing."

"It's not nothing!" Maya heard her own voice rise, felt the panic clawing at her throat. "Something is wrong with me.

Something is really, really wrong, and you're acting like this is all completely normal."

"It is normal. For you."

Maya went still.

"What do you mean, 'for me'?"

Mira sighed. "Maya, we've talked about this before. Years ago. You don't remember because you never remember—that's how it works. But this isn't new. This has been happening your whole life."

"What has been happening my whole life?"

"The gaps. The lost time. The moments when you're... not quite yourself." Mira's voice was gentle, almost tender. "I've always been here to cover for you. To make sure things run smoothly when you're not available. That's what sisters do."

Maya felt the room tilt around her. "Are you saying this is some kind of... condition? That I have blackouts and you just never told me?"

"I'm saying that you're not as present as you think you are. You never have been. And that's okay—I pick up the slack. I always have. But you can't fall apart about it now, not with the journalist sniffing around, not with everything we've built at stake."

"Mira—"

"Go teach your class. Eat something. Drink water. Take a bath tonight and go to bed early. The memories will come back, or they won't—it doesn't matter. What matters is that you keep showing up. Keep being Maya. I'll handle the rest."

"I don't understand what you're telling me."

"You don't have to understand. You just have to trust me."

The line went dead.

Maya sat in her office, staring at the phone in her hand. Her sister's words echoed in her head, rearranging themselves into patterns she couldn't quite grasp.

This has been happening your whole life.
You're not as present as you think you are.
I'll handle the rest.

She thought about the day she'd lost. The classes she'd taught without remembering. The texts she'd sent in her own voice from fingers she didn't recall moving.

She thought about her hair, loose and soft when she woke up. The way Mira always wore her hair.

She thought about how she never saw her sister. How they never appeared in the same photographs. How every time she tried to remember the last time they'd been in the same room, the memory slipped away like water through her fingers.

A terrible thought began to form at the edges of her mind. A thought so impossible, so horrifying, that she pushed it away before it could fully take shape.

She was just stressed. Just tired. Just losing time the way people sometimes did when they had too much on their plates.

There was nothing wrong with her. There was nothing wrong with any of this.

Mira was real. Mira was her sister. Mira would come over again soon, and they would talk, and everything would make sense.

Maya stood up from her desk. She had a class to teach in an hour. Students who needed her. An empire that needed its face.

She checked her reflection in the window. Hair up. Makeup fresh. Ankle bracelet catching the light.

She looked like Maya Sharma. She would be Maya Sharma.

Whatever else was happening—whatever gaps were opening in her memory, whatever voice was whispering terrible questions in the back of her mind—she would deal with it later.

Right now, she had a performance to give.

And if there was one thing Maya Sharma knew how to do, it was perform.

8

Mira
The Business
The same Tuesday that Maya lost.

The woman in the mirror wore her hair down.

She had woken early—before dawn, before the city stirred—and moved through the apartment with the quiet efficiency that came naturally to her. Shower. Meditation. The careful ritual of becoming.

Today required Maya. The staff meeting, the power vinyasa class, the interview prep, the donor session. A full day of being seen, being charming, being the face that launched a thousand wellness retreats.

But Maya wasn't available.

Maya had been slipping lately. The stress of the journalist, the unresolved tension with their mother, the cracks that were beginning to show in the carefully constructed foundation of their shared life. Sometimes, when the pressure built too high, Maya simply... went away. Retreated to some inner room that Mira couldn't access, leaving her body behind like an empty house.

When that happened, someone had to step in.

Someone always had to step in.

Mira—no, not Mira today, today she was Maya—pulled her hair back into a sleek ponytail. Applied makeup with a heavier hand than she preferred: defined brows, bronzer, tinted lip. Chose clothes from the left side of the closet, the side she rarely touched: fitted black leggings, a crimson tank top that showed her shoulders, the gold ankle bracelet that felt foreign against her skin.

She looked in the mirror and practiced the smile. Bright. Warm. Inviting.

"Good morning," she said to her reflection, pitching her voice slightly higher than usual. "So glad you could make it. Let's transform together."

The words felt like stones in her mouth. But she'd had decades of practice. She could be Maya for a day. She'd been Maya many times before.

The staff meeting was easy. She'd attended enough of them as herself—quiet in the corner, taking notes, watching Maya command the room—that she knew the rhythms. The jokes Maya made, the way she touched people's shoulders when she praised them, the specific cadence of her inspirational tangents.

"I want us to think about what we're really offering here," she said, standing at the head of the table while the staff watched with eager eyes. "It's not yoga. It's not fitness. It's not even wellness, really. What we're offering is permission. Permission to slow down. Permission to feel. Permission to become who they've always been underneath all the armor."

Heads nodded. Someone took notes. Devi, the studio manager, beamed at her with something like worship.

It was so easy to make them love her. To make them believe.

All she had to do was say the words Maya would say, in the voice Maya would use, with the confidence Maya projected like a force field.

The real Maya struggled with confidence. The real Maya needed constant reassurance, constant validation, constant proof that she was enough. That was why she performed so well—she was always desperately trying to earn what Mira simply knew how to take.

But they didn't see that. They saw the mask, and the mask was flawless.

After the meeting, she retreated to Maya's office to prepare for the noon class. Power vinyasa. Ninety minutes of heat and sweat and relentless forward motion. Not her preferred style—she liked the slow practices, the quiet unfolding, the surrender of yin and restorative. But she could do this. She could do anything when she had to.

She reviewed Maya's playlist. Upbeat, driving, carefully designed to peak at exactly the right moment. She reviewed the sequence Maya had planned—a progression from grounding poses through standing strength work to a challenging peak of arm balances, then a slow descent into stillness.

It was a good sequence. Maya was good at this, when she was present. The problem was that Maya was present less and less often.

At 11:45, she walked into the studio. Forty students were already there, mats arranged in neat rows, water bottles stationed at corners, faces eager with anticipation. They looked at her—at Maya—with the particular hunger of people who wanted to be saved.

She smiled at them. That bright, Maya smile.

"Welcome," she said. "Let's begin."

. . .

The class was a blur of breath and movement.

She moved through the sequence on autopilot, calling poses, offering adjustments, delivering the little motivational gems that Maya was famous for. "Find your edge." "Breathe through the resistance." "The obstacle is the path."

The students responded beautifully. They always did. They pushed harder, reached deeper, surrendered more completely. By the time she brought them into the final relaxation, half the room was trembling with exhaustion, and several people were quietly weeping.

"You did the work today," she said, walking among them as they lay in savasana. "You showed up for yourselves. That's all any of us can do. Show up. Again and again. Even when it's hard. Especially when it's hard."

She meant it, in her own way. Showing up was everything. Being present, being reliable, being the one who held things together when everyone else fell apart.

That was what she did. What she'd always done.

After class, a young woman approached her with tears still wet on her cheeks.

"Thank you," she said, grabbing Maya's hands with desperate intensity. "I've been coming to your classes for a year, and I've never felt anything like that. You just... you see me. You really see me."

The words triggered something. A memory, or the echo of a memory. Another young woman, years ago, saying almost exactly the same thing. *You see me. You really see me.*

What had happened to that woman? She couldn't quite remember. There had been some complication. Some problem that needed handling.

She had handled it. She always handled things.

"I'm so glad," she said to the student, squeezing her hands

warmly. "That's what we're here for. To see each other. To hold space for each other's becoming."

The woman nodded, eyes shining, and floated away on a cloud of endorphins and spiritual validation.

Mira—Maya—watched her go with an expression of serene compassion.

Inside, she felt nothing at all.

The publicist meeting was straightforward. Angela Chen, a sharp woman in her forties who had been handling Prana & Bones' media presence for three years, wanted to discuss strategy for the upcoming *Wellspring* profile.

"I'm a little concerned about this journalist," Angela said, tapping a pen against her notebook. "Celeste Park. She's got a background in investigative work. Left the *Tribune* after some budget cuts, but before that, she was doing serious pieces. Exposés. Takedowns."

"She seemed harmless enough when I met her," Maya's voice said. "Standard wellness profile questions. Nothing unusual."

"Maybe. But I did some digging, and there's something interesting." Angela slid a printout across the desk. "She had a sister. Younger sister named Bree Park. Bree attended one of your Tulum retreats about four years ago."

A cold feeling spread through her chest. She kept her face perfectly still.

"We've had thousands of students," she said. "I can't be expected to remember everyone."

"Of course not. But here's the thing—Bree Park basically disappeared about six months after that retreat. Dropped off social media, disconnected her phone, stopped contacting family. Celeste has been looking for her for years."

"That's very sad, but I'm not sure what it has to do with us."

"Probably nothing. I just wanted you to be aware. If this journalist has a personal axe to grind—if she blames the retreat for her sister's... whatever happened to her sister—we need to be prepared for that angle."

"What do you suggest?"

"Be careful. Be transparent. Don't give her anything that could be twisted." Angela gathered her materials and stood. "And maybe... I don't know. Do you have any records from that retreat? Waivers, contact information? It might be worth knowing what this Bree person signed up for, what she participated in, whether there's any documentation we should be aware of."

"I'll look into it," Maya's voice said smoothly. "Thank you, Angela. You're always so thorough."

After the publicist left, she sat alone in the office for a long moment.

Bree Park.

The name rose from the depths of memory like a corpse floating to the surface of a lake.

She remembered now. The eager young woman at the Tulum retreat. The one who had attached herself to Maya—to the real Maya—with alarming intensity. The one who had started showing up at the studio afterward, attending every class, volunteering for every event, sending long emails full of gratitude and need.

The one who had become a problem.

She had handled that problem. Quietly, carefully, the way she handled all problems. A gentle redirection. A suggestion that Bree's spiritual journey might benefit from a more intensive experience—an ashram overseas, a silent retreat, somewhere far away where her hunger could be someone else's concern.

It had worked. Bree had drifted out of their orbit, following the breadcrumbs laid for her. Last she'd heard, the woman was somewhere in Southeast Asia, chasing enlightenment in the way that broken women often did.

But now Bree's sister was here. Asking questions. Looking for answers that couldn't be given.

This was a problem. A significant one.

She pulled out her phone and composed a text—not to Maya's contacts, but to her own. To the encrypted app she used for communications that needed to stay private.

B.P.'s sister is the journalist. Personal vendetta. Need to assess threat level.

The response came within minutes, from a contact listed only as a single initial: *K.*

Understood. What do you need?

Everything you can find on Celeste Park. Movements, contacts, vulnerabilities. And see if there's any trail on B.P.—where she ended up, whether she's still alive, whether she's been in contact with anyone.

Timeline?

Yesterday.

She put the phone away and stood up. One more appointment: the donor session with the Greenwell Foundation representative. Then she could let Maya take back over. Let her wake up tomorrow with no memory of today, convinced that she'd simply been tired, simply been stressed, simply been overworked.

That was the arrangement. That was how they survived.

Maya existed for the world to love. Mira existed to do what Maya couldn't.

And when there were problems—when there were complications, threats, people who got too close to truths that couldn't be spoken—Mira handled them.

She always had.
She always would.

The Greenwell donor was a wealthy woman in her sixties named Patricia, who had discovered yoga after her husband's death and now wanted to give away portions of his fortune to organizations that aligned with her newfound spiritual values.

"I just feel so transformed," Patricia said, clutching a cup of ceremonial-grade matcha. "The practice has given me a whole new lease on life. I want to share that with others. I want to fund scholarships for people who couldn't otherwise afford this experience."

"That's beautiful," Maya's voice said warmly. "We're so aligned in that vision. Yoga shouldn't be a luxury—it should be accessible to everyone."

"Exactly! Exactly." Patricia beamed. "I knew you'd understand. From the moment I took your class, I knew we were kindred spirits."

The conversation continued in that vein for another hour. By the end, Patricia had committed to a monthly sponsorship that would fund ten scholarships per year, plus a significant donation to the studio's expansion fund.

It was, by any measure, a successful meeting. Another wealthy person converted, another revenue stream secured, another brick in the wall of the empire.

But as she walked Patricia to the elevator, something caught her attention.

A woman standing across the street, half-hidden behind a parked car. Watching the building. Watching her.

Dark hair. Sharp features. A leather bag over one shoulder.

Celeste Park.

Their eyes met for just a moment. Then the journalist

turned and walked away, disappearing into the flow of pedestrian traffic.

She had been watched. Followed. Observed.

The journalist was no longer just asking questions. She was hunting.

Back in the office, she pulled out her phone and composed another message:

She's surveilling the studio. This has escalated beyond a profile. Need to accelerate timeline on information gathering. And start thinking about contingencies.

The response came quickly:

What kind of contingencies?

She considered the question for a long moment. Then she typed:

The kind that make problems go away permanently.

She sent the message, then deleted the entire conversation. Removed the app. Reset the phone to factory settings.

When Maya woke up tomorrow, there would be no trace of what had been discussed, what had been planned, what had been set in motion.

Maya would remember nothing.

That was the point of Maya. That was what Maya was for.

To be innocent. To be ignorant. To have clean hands while the dirty work happened in the shadows.

And if the dirty work got dirtier—if the contingencies became necessary—well.

That was what Mira was for too.

That night, she went home to Mira's apartment, not Maya's. She let her hair down, changed into soft clothes, washed Maya off her skin in a scalding shower.

In the closet, she opened the wooden box with the brass

latch. The index cards waited inside, patient and orderly. She found the one she was looking for:

Bree P. — 6/8/2021 — extreme need for validation, unstable attachment, potential risk

She added a new note to the back of the card:

Sister is journalist C. Park. Investigating. Potentially dangerous. Monitor.

Then she pulled out a fresh card and wrote:

Celeste Park — surveilling studio — personal connection to B.P. — threat level: HIGH

She filed both cards away and closed the box.

Tomorrow, Maya would wake up confused, fragmented, struggling to understand the gaps in her memory. She would call Mira in a panic, and Mira would soothe her, reassure her, tell her everything was fine.

And everything would be fine. Because Mira would make sure of it.

That was what sisters were for.

9

Celeste
The Sister

The photograph was wearing thin at the edges.

Celeste had handled it too many times over the years—picking it up, putting it down, tracing the outline of Bree's face with her fingertip as if she could somehow reach through the glossy surface and pull her sister back into the world. The colors had faded slightly, the way photographs did when exposed to too much light, too much touch, too much longing.

She sat on her bed at 2 AM, unable to sleep, the photograph balanced on her knee.

Bree at the airport. Bree with her overstuffed backpack and her wide smile. Bree on her way to find herself, not knowing she would lose herself instead.

Four years. Four years of searching, of dead ends, of conversations that went nowhere. Four years of private investigators who took her money and returned with nothing. Four years of police reports filed and ignored, of missing persons databases that yielded no matches, of lying awake at night imagining all the terrible things that might have happened to her baby sister.

And now, finally, a thread.

Celeste set down the photograph and picked up her laptop. She'd been compiling everything she'd gathered since the interview with Maya Sharma, organizing it into a document that was starting to look less like research for a profile and more like evidence for a case.

PRANA & BONES - INVESTIGATION NOTES

The Sisters

- Maya Sharma: public face, charismatic, omnipresent in media
- Mira Sharma: largely invisible, handles "business side"
- No photographs of them together (confirmed across 500+ images)
- Staff report never seeing them in same room
- Jonah Whitfield: "I don't think there are two of them"

Inconsistencies

- Maya's training records: claims Mysore 2008, no verification
- Origin story (abusive boyfriend): possibly fabricated? Source TBD
- Multiple reports of Maya "not recognizing" longtime staff/students
- Reports of personality shifts, different "energy" on different days

Bree

- Attended Tulum retreat June 2021
- Last normal contact: September 2021
- Mentioned "Maya sees me" - singular, not plural
- Disappeared approximately 6 months post-retreat
- Last known location: possibly Southeast Asia?

Questions

- What happened at the Tulum retreat?
- Who else has disappeared after involvement with P&B?

- What is Mira's actual role?
- Are Maya and Mira the same person?

That last question still felt insane when she looked at it written out. Two sisters running a business together, never photographed together, never seen in the same room—the simplest explanation was that they were private, that they had unusual boundaries, that the wellness industry attracted eccentric personalities.

But Celeste had spent too many years as a journalist to believe in simple explanations. Simple explanations were what people gave you when they wanted you to stop asking questions.

She pulled up her email and checked for new responses to her interview requests. Three more former employees had declined to comment. One had blocked her entirely. But there was a new message, received just an hour ago, from an address she didn't recognize:

From: truthseeker2019@protonmail.com **Subject:** You're asking the right questions

Ms. Park,

I know what you're looking for. I know about your sister. I know about the others too.

They're not going to talk to you. The ones who left—they're too scared. The ones who stayed—they're too far gone. But I have information. Documents. Proof.

If you want the truth about Prana & Bones, meet me Friday at 11 PM. There's a parking garage on West 38th Street, between 8th and 9th Avenue. Top level. Come alone.

Don't respond to this email. It won't exist in an hour.

And Ms. Park? Be careful. They're watching you. They've been watching you since the interview.

—A friend

Celeste read the message three times.

It could be a trap. It probably was a trap. Anonymous emails, parking garages at night, instructions to come alone—this was how journalists ended up dead in movies, and occasionally in real life.

But "the others too."

That phrase snagged in her mind like a fishhook. The others. Not just Bree. Others.

How many people had disappeared into the orbit of Prana & Bones? How many families were out there right now, doing what Celeste had been doing for four years—searching, hoping, slowly losing their minds with grief and uncertainty?

She thought about Jonah Whitfield, his career destroyed by anonymous accusations. She thought about the other former employees who wouldn't return her calls. She thought about the journalist Angela had mentioned in passing—the wellness blogger who had started asking questions years ago and then suddenly stopped.

A pattern. She was seeing the edges of a pattern, and she needed to know how deep it went.

She checked the clock. It was Wednesday now—or Thursday, technically. The meeting was Friday night. She had two days to prepare.

She started a new document:

FRIDAY MEETING - PRECAUTIONS
- Tell someone where I'm going (who?)
- Arrive early, scope the location
- Bring phone, keep it on, share location with...
- Pepper spray? Taser? (check legality)
- Have exit strategy
- Record everything

She paused at "tell someone where I'm going." Who could she tell? Her editor would think she was crazy. Her mother would panic. Her friends—the few she had left after years of obsessive searching for Bree—would try to talk her out of it.

There was no one. She would have to go alone, truly alone, and hope that whoever was waiting for her in that parking garage actually wanted to help.

She closed the laptop and lay back on her bed, staring at the ceiling.

Bree's face floated in her mind. The last time she'd seen her, two years ago. Too thin, too bright, talking about Maya Sharma like she was some kind of messiah.

You don't understand. You've never understood. Maya sees me. She really sees me.

"I'm trying," Celeste whispered to the empty room. "I'm trying to understand. I'm trying to find you. Just hold on a little longer. Please."

The ceiling didn't answer.

She picked up the photograph again and pressed it to her chest, curling around it like a child with a stuffed animal.

Tomorrow, she would be a journalist again—rational, methodical, following the evidence wherever it led. But tonight, in the dark, she was just a sister who missed her sister.

A sister who would do anything to bring her home.

The next day, Celeste threw herself into preparation.

She researched the parking garage—a public structure with 24-hour access, security cameras in the stairwells but not on the top level. She drove by it twice, memorizing the exits, noting the surrounding businesses that would be closed at 11 PM on a Friday night.

She bought pepper spray from a bodega that didn't ask questions. She charged a portable battery pack and tested her phone's voice recording app. She wrote a letter—to her mother, to be opened if she didn't come back—and sealed it in an envelope that she hid in her desk drawer.

She told no one. There was no one to tell.

But she also kept investigating, because she couldn't stop, because stopping meant giving up, and giving up meant accepting that Bree was gone forever.

She tracked down more former students from the Tulum retreat Bree had attended. Most didn't respond to her messages. Two agreed to talk, but only by phone, and only on the condition that she not use their names.

The first was a woman named Jessica, who had attended the retreat for her thirtieth birthday.

"It was intense," Jessica said, her voice careful and measured. "More intense than I expected. They really push you to open up, to share your deepest fears, your traumas. By day three, I was crying in front of strangers about things I'd never told anyone."

"Did that feel manipulative to you?"

"At the time? No. It felt liberating. Like I was finally being seen, finally being heard. But afterward..." Jessica paused. "Afterward, I felt kind of... empty. Like I'd given away something I couldn't get back. And they kept reaching out, you know? Emails, invitations to more retreats, more trainings. It felt less like community and more like... I don't know. Hunger."

"Do you remember a woman named Bree Park? She would have been at the same retreat."

"Bree..." Jessica was quiet for a moment. "Small, dark hair, really intense energy? Always wanted to sit next to Maya during the sharing circles?"

Celeste's heart hammered. "That sounds like her."

"Yeah, I remember her. She was... she got really deep into it. Like, deeper than most of us. By the end of the retreat, she was talking about quitting her job, moving to be closer to the studio, dedicating her life to 'the work.'" Jessica's voice dropped. "I remember thinking it was a little much. But I also remember thinking Maya encouraged it. Encouraged her specifically. Like she saw something in Bree that the rest of us didn't have."

"What do you think she saw?"

"I don't know. Vulnerability, maybe. Desperation. Bree was looking for something—really looking, in a way that most of us weren't. Most of us just wanted to relax, do some yoga, maybe have a breakthrough or two. But Bree wanted to be transformed. She wanted to be completely different than she was."

"And Maya picked up on that."

"Maya picks up on everything. That's what makes her so good at what she does." Jessica paused. "And so dangerous, if you're the wrong kind of person."

The second call was with a man named Derek, who had attended the retreat with his then-girlfriend.

"We broke up three months after we got back," Derek said bluntly. "She got really into the Prana & Bones thing—started going to the studio every day, spending all her money on trainings and supplements. I told her it felt like a cult, and she said I just didn't understand. Said I was 'spiritually closed.' Said Maya had helped her see that our relationship was 'holding her back from her evolution.'"

"Those exact words?"

"Exact words. I remember because I'd never heard her talk like that before. It was like she'd been given a new vocabulary, a new way of seeing the world, and I wasn't part of it anymore."

"Do you know what happened to her? After you broke up?"

"Not really. We're not in touch. Last I heard, she was doing one of their teacher trainings, planning to open her own studio." Derek laughed bitterly. "Franchise model, you know? They train you, you open a studio, you give them a cut. It's genius, really. Build an army of believers and monetize their faith."

"Did you ever meet Mira? Maya's sister?"

"The other one?" Derek considered. "I saw her once, I think. At the studio, teaching some kind of mellow class. Yin or restorative or whatever. But I never talked to her. She kept to herself."

"Did you ever see Maya and Mira together?"

A long pause.

"You know what's weird? I don't think I did. I just assumed they were both there, you know? But now that you mention it..." Derek trailed off. "Huh. That is weird, isn't it?"

After the calls, Celeste sat with her notes, trying to piece together a picture from the fragments.

Bree had been vulnerable. Seeking. The exact kind of person Maya Sharma seemed to target—or attract, depending on how you looked at it. She had gone deep into the Prana & Bones world, deeper than most, encouraged by Maya herself.

And then she had disappeared.

What had happened in the six months between the retreat and Bree's final message? What had Bree gotten involved in? What had she seen, or learned, or become?

Celeste pulled up her sister's old social media accounts—the ones she had memorized, the ones she checked religiously even though they hadn't been updated in years.

Bree's final Instagram post was from September 2021. A photo of a sunset over water, location tagged as Tulum, Mexico. The caption read:

Sometimes you have to lose yourself to find yourself. Grateful for this journey, for these teachers, for the path that's unfolding. The old Bree is gone. The new one is just beginning. 🙏 🌅

The comments were full of heart emojis and "so inspiring!" and "living your best life!" Nobody had noticed anything wrong. Nobody had seen the warning signs that seemed so obvious in retrospect.

The old Bree is gone.

At the time, Celeste had thought it was just wellness-speak. The kind of thing people said when they'd had a transformative experience, when they wanted to signal that they'd changed, that they'd grown.

Now, looking at the words through the lens of everything she'd learned, they read differently.

Like a goodbye.

Like a warning.

Like a confession.

Celeste closed the laptop and pressed her hands over her eyes, fighting back the tears that threatened to spill.

One more day until the meeting. One more day until she might finally get some answers.

She didn't know what she would find in that parking garage. Didn't know if the anonymous emailer was a friend or a threat or something in between.

But she was going to find out.

For Bree. For all the others.

For herself.

10

Maya
The Mother

The voicemail had been sitting in her phone for three days.

Maya stared at it every morning—that small notification, that red badge that refused to go away. *Sunita Sharma. 3:47 PM. 2 minutes, 34 seconds.* Longer than her mother's usual messages, which were typically brief and businesslike. *Just checking in. Hope you're well. Call me when you can.*

This one was different. Maya could feel it without even pressing play. Something in the weight of it, the length of it, the way it sat in her phone like a stone she couldn't swallow.

She'd been avoiding it since Tuesday. Since waking up on the bathroom floor with no memory of Wednesday and a growing terror that something was deeply, fundamentally wrong with her.

Mira had told her not to worry. Mira had told her this was normal—for her. But Mira wasn't answering her calls anymore. Three days of texts that went unanswered, calls that rang through to voicemail, a silence that felt less like privacy and more like abandonment.

She's busy, Maya told herself. *She's handling things. She's always handling things.*

But the voice in the back of her mind—the one she'd been trying to silence since Thursday morning—whispered something else.

When did you last see her?

Actually see her. In the flesh. Not a voice on the phone. Not a text on a screen. When did you last look into her eyes?

Maya couldn't remember. The dinner on Tuesday night was vivid in her mind—the pasta, the wine, the conversation about their mother—but when she tried to picture Mira sitting across from her, the image blurred. She could see the kitchen table, the candles, the plates of food. But Mira's face kept slipping away, like trying to hold water in her hands.

That was just stress. Just exhaustion. Just the gaps in her memory bleeding into everything, making her doubt things she shouldn't doubt.

Mira was real. Mira was her sister. Mira had been at dinner on Tuesday night.

Hadn't she?

Maya pressed play on the voicemail.

Her mother's voice filled the room, and immediately she knew something was wrong. Sunita sounded older than Maya remembered. Tired. And underneath the tiredness, something else—a tremor that might have been fear.

"Maya, beta. It's Mom. I know you don't want to talk to me. I know you think I'm—" A pause. A shaky breath. "I know what you think. But I need you to listen. Please. Just this once."

Maya sank onto the edge of her bed, phone pressed to her ear.

"I talked to Mira yesterday. She called me, the way she

always does. Every Sunday, like clockwork. She tells me about the business, about you, about how everything is fine. And I listen, and I play along, because what else can I do? What else can I do when my daughter won't—"

Another pause. Longer this time. Maya could hear her mother composing herself, gathering the words.

"But yesterday was different. She said things, Maya. Things that scared me. About a journalist who's asking questions. About problems that need to be handled. About making sure the business is protected no matter what."

Maya's blood went cold.

"I've heard her talk like that before. Years ago, when you were just starting out. When that woman—the one whose story you told—when she tried to contact you. Do you remember what happened to her, Maya? Do you remember what Mira said she would do?"

Maya didn't remember. That was the problem. She never remembered.

"I've been so scared for so long. Scared to push you, scared to say the wrong thing, scared that if I tell you what I really think, you'll disappear completely. But I can't stay quiet anymore. Not with what Mira said yesterday. Not with that tone in her voice."

Sunita's voice cracked.

"Maya, listen to me. I need you to hear this, really hear it, even if you can't understand it right now. Even if it sounds crazy. Even if you think I've lost my mind."

A long, terrible pause.

"There is something wrong. There has been something wrong since you were nine years old, since your father died, since that day at the overlook when everything changed. I've watched it for thirty-four years. I've tried to help. I've tried to get you to see someone, to talk to someone, to understand what's happening inside your own mind. But you won't listen. You never listen. And now I'm afraid it's too late."

Maya realized she was crying. Tears streaming down her face, silent and hot.

"The journalist—whoever she is—she's going to find things. Things that can't be explained. Things that will raise questions you're not ready to answer. And when that happens, Mira is going to do what Mira always does. She's going to protect you. She's going to *handle* it."

Her mother's voice dropped to a whisper.

"But Maya, beta, you have to understand something. You have to hear this even if you can't believe it."

The words came slow and clear, each one a nail being driven into Maya's chest.

"Mira can't protect you from yourself. No one can protect you from yourself. Because the things Mira does, the things she's always done—"

A sob. Her mother was crying now too.

"Those are your hands, Maya. They've always been your hands."

The voicemail ended.

Maya sat frozen on the edge of her bed, the phone still pressed to her ear, listening to nothing. The silence roared.

Those are your hands.

She looked down at her fingers. The familiar gold ring on her right hand. The neat manicure she maintained religiously. The small scar on her left thumb from a kitchen accident years ago.

Her hands. Her ordinary, familiar hands.

What had they done?

What had Mira made them do?

No, she corrected herself. *What has Mira done? Mira is sepa-*

rate. Mira is her own person. Mira handles things because Maya can't, because Maya is too soft, too weak, too—

But the voice in her mind wouldn't stop.

When did you last see her?
Why aren't there any photographs?
Why does Mom sound so scared?
Why can't you remember?

Maya stood up abruptly, her body moving before her mind could catch up. She needed to do something. She needed to talk to Mira, to confront her, to demand an explanation for whatever her mother was implying.

She called Mira's number. It rang four times, then went to voicemail.

"Hey, this is Mira. Leave a message."

Such a simple greeting. Such a familiar voice. Maya had heard it thousands of times—on the phone, across dinner tables, in the studio hallways. It was her sister's voice. Different from her own. Softer, lower, with that particular quality that made people feel safe.

Wasn't it different from her own?

She'd never really thought about it before. Never had reason to. Of course Mira sounded like herself. Of course Maya sounded like Maya. They were sisters, not the same person.

But now, listening to the voicemail greeting, Maya felt something shift in her perception. Like one of those optical illusions where you suddenly see the hidden image and can never unsee it again.

The voice on Mira's voicemail.

It sounded like Maya's voice.

Not identical. Softer, yes. Lower, yes. But the cadence, the rhythm, the particular way certain words were shaped—it was the same. The same voice, pitched slightly differently. The same voice, coming from the same throat.

No. No, no, no.

Maya ended the call without leaving a message. Her hands were shaking so badly she almost dropped the phone.

This was insane. She was being insane. Her mother's voicemail had gotten into her head, planted seeds of doubt that were now flowering into full-blown paranoia.

Mira was real. Mira had her own apartment, her own life, her own closet full of soft clothes and silver jewelry. Maya had been there—had visited, had spent time in that space. She could picture it clearly: the white walls, the single orchid, the meditation cushion by the window.

Could she picture it?

She tried to summon the memory and found it strangely vague. She knew the apartment existed. She knew what it looked like. But when she tried to remember actually *being* there—walking through the door, sitting on the couch, having a conversation with Mira in that space—the images dissolved like smoke.

Maybe she'd never been to Mira's apartment.

Maybe she'd only heard it described. Only imagined it. Only built a picture in her mind from details Mira had mentioned over the phone.

Or maybe she'd been there many times, in states she couldn't remember. Maybe she'd walked through that door and become someone else. Maybe the apartment felt familiar because it was *hers*—another life she was living without knowing it.

Maya pressed her palms against her eyes until she saw stars.

She needed to know. She needed to see for herself.

She grabbed her keys from the hook by the door—and froze.

There was an extra key on her keyring.

She hadn't noticed it before, or maybe she'd noticed it and

not registered it, the way you stop seeing things that are always there. But now it seemed to glow in her palm, demanding attention.

A silver key. Newer than the others. No label, no marking, nothing to indicate what it opened.

Maya stared at it.

She knew where Mira lived. Knew the address, the building, the apartment number. She'd sent packages there, had things delivered, knew the cross streets and the nearest subway stop.

Did this key open that door?

There was one way to find out.

The building was a brownstone on a tree-lined street in Brooklyn. Beautiful in a way that suggested money without screaming it. Maya had never been here before—she was certain of that, almost certain, as certain as she could be about anything anymore.

She climbed the stairs to the third floor. Apartment 3B. The door was dark wood, unremarkable, identical to all the others in the hallway.

She raised her hand to knock.

Then she lowered it.

If Mira was home, Maya would have to explain why she was here. Would have to admit to the doubts, the fears, the terrible suspicions that had been growing since her mother's voicemail. She would have to look her sister in the eye and ask: *Are you real? Am I losing my mind? What are you doing with my hands when I'm not there to watch?*

She couldn't do that. Not yet. Not until she knew more.

Instead, she pulled out the silver key and slid it into the lock.

It fit perfectly.

The door swung open.

Maya stepped inside and felt the world tilt beneath her feet.

She knew this place.

Not from visiting—she was certain now that she'd never consciously been here before. But her body knew it. Her feet knew exactly how many steps from the door to the bedroom. Her hand reached for the light switch in the precise spot where it waited on the wall.

The apartment was Mira's. The muted colors, the minimal furniture, the single orchid on the windowsill. The sandalwood scent that hung in the air like a ghost.

But it was also hers. The layout was a mirror of her own apartment—same bones, different skin. And everywhere she looked, she saw echoes of herself. A sweater she thought she'd lost months ago, draped over a chair. A book she'd been meaning to read, sitting on the nightstand. A mug in the sink that was identical to one in her own kitchen.

How is this possible?

She moved through the space like a sleepwalker, touching things, confirming their reality. The furniture was real. The clothes in the closet were real. The jewelry on the dresser was real—Mira's rings, Mira's necklaces, all the silver and stone that Maya had seen on her sister's hands and throat.

She'd seen them.

Hadn't she?

Or had she only ever seen them in mirrors?

Maya's breath was coming fast now. Too fast. She forced herself to slow down, to think, to approach this like a problem that could be solved.

There had to be an explanation. Maybe Mira had borrowed her things. Maybe they'd bought duplicates of items they both liked. Maybe the sense of familiarity was just because they were sisters with similar taste, not because—

Not because—

She couldn't finish the thought.

The closet. She needed to see the closet.

She didn't know why, but she knew with sudden certainty that the closet held answers. Something was waiting for her there, behind the hanging clothes, in the darkness at the back.

She crossed the room. Opened the closet door. Pushed aside the soft fabrics—cream and gray and sage, all the colors she never wore but somehow recognized.

There was a shelf built into the back wall.

On the shelf were three boxes.

Maya's hands moved without her permission, reaching for the first box. Small. Covered in worn velvet. She opened it.

Jewelry.

Dozens of pieces. Rings, earrings, necklaces, bracelets. Some were expensive, some were cheap. None of them were Mira's usual style.

Each piece had a small tag attached. A name and a date, written in careful handwriting.

Sarah M. — 4/12/2019 Jennifer L. — 7/3/2020 Diana K. — 2/14/2022

Maya recognized the handwriting.

It was her own.

She dropped the box. Jewelry scattered across the closet floor, glinting in the dim light like eyes.

The second box. Wooden. Brass latch.

She shouldn't open it. She should leave, right now, should walk out of this apartment and never come back. Should call someone—a doctor, a therapist, the police. Should do anything except open this box and see what was inside.

Her hands opened the box anyway.

Index cards. Hundreds of them, held together with rubber

bands. Each card had a name, a date, and notes in that same familiar handwriting.

Jennifer M. — 3/15/2019 — grief, recent divorce, desperate for connection. Easy.

David O. — 7/22/2020 — anxiety disorder, seeking meaning, very susceptible. Gave too much. Had to redirect.

Paula R. — 11/3/2021 — childhood trauma, authority issues, would do anything for approval. Potential problem. Handled.

Handled.

Maya flipped through the cards with numb fingers. Dozens of names. Dozens of assessments. Dozens of people who had passed through Prana & Bones and been catalogued like specimens, their vulnerabilities noted, their usefulness measured.

And then, near the bottom of the stack, a card that stopped her heart.

Bree P. — 6/8/2021 — extreme need for validation, unstable attachment, potential risk. Redirected to ashram. Handled permanently.

Handled permanently.

What did that mean? What had happened to Bree P.? What had—

Her fingers found another card. Older. The paper yellowed, the handwriting younger but still recognizably her own.

Maya S. — created to carry the softness. Doesn't know she's not real. Keep her sleeping.

Maya read the words three times.

They didn't make sense. They couldn't make sense. She was Maya. She was real. She was standing here, in this apartment, reading this card, with her own two eyes and her own two hands—

Her hands.

Those are your hands, Maya. They've always been your hands.

There was a third box.

She didn't want to open it. Every instinct screamed at her to stop, to run, to pretend she'd never found this place. But her hands were already moving, already reaching, already pulling the third box from the shelf.

It was five times larger than the others. Heavier. More like a trunk.

She opened it.

Shoes.

Single left shoes, arranged in neat rows. Sandals, sneakers, heels, flats. Some were old—the leather cracked, the soles worn thin. Some were newer, barely scuffed. All of them left shoes. Dozens of them. Maybe fifty. Maybe more.

Each shoe had a tag.

Names. Dates.

The oldest tag was from 2003. Over twenty years ago.

Maya sank to the floor of the closet, surrounded by jewelry and index cards and single left shoes, and finally understood.

There was no Mira.

There had never been a Mira.

There was only her. Only Maya. Only this fractured mind that had been splitting and splitting for decades, creating new selves to handle what the original couldn't bear.

The jewelry was hers. The cards were hers. The shoes were hers.

The hands that had collected them—that had taken pieces of people, catalogued their weaknesses, *handled* the ones who became problems—

Those were her hands.

They had always been her hands.

Maya opened her mouth to scream.

No sound came out.

And somewhere in the darkness at the back of her mind, something that called itself Mira opened its eyes and smiled.

11

Celeste
The Parking Garage

The top level of the parking garage was empty except for three cars and a thousand shadows.

Celeste had arrived twenty minutes early, as planned. She'd walked the perimeter twice, noted the exits, tested her phone's signal strength, and confirmed that her location was being shared with a cloud account she'd set up specifically for this purpose. If something happened to her tonight, someone would eventually find the breadcrumbs.

The question was whether "eventually" would be soon enough.

It was 10:47 PM. The city hummed below her, muffled by concrete and distance. Up here, the only sounds were the occasional groan of the building settling and the whisper of wind through the open sides of the structure.

She'd chosen a position near the stairwell—close enough to run if she needed to, far enough from the elevator that she'd have warning if someone approached that way. Her pepper spray was in her right pocket. Her phone was recording in her left. Her heart was pounding so hard she could feel it in her teeth.

This is insane, she thought for the hundredth time. *This is how people get killed.*

But the email had promised proof. Documents. Information about others who had disappeared into the orbit of Prana & Bones.

For Bree, she would risk insanity. For Bree, she would risk anything.

10:52 PM.

A car engine somewhere below. Celeste tensed, tracking the sound as it wound up through the levels of the garage. Headlights swept across the concrete pillars, casting long shadows that stretched and retreated like grasping fingers.

The car emerged onto the top level. A dark sedan, nondescript, the kind of vehicle designed to be forgotten. It pulled into a spot thirty feet from where Celeste stood and killed its lights.

For a long moment, nothing happened.

Then the driver's door opened, and a woman stepped out.

She was older than Celeste had expected—mid-fifties, maybe, with graying hair pulled back in a severe bun and a face that looked like it had been carved from exhaustion. She wore a dark coat despite the mild weather, and she moved with the careful deliberation of someone who had learned that the world was full of threats.

"Ms. Park?" The woman's voice was low, rough, like she'd spent years not using it.

"That's me." Celeste didn't move from her position. "And you are?"

"Someone who made the same mistake you're making." The woman stopped about ten feet away, keeping distance between them. "Someone who asked questions about Prana &

Bones and learned what happens to people who dig too deep."

"You're the journalist. From Arizona."

A flicker of surprise crossed the woman's face. "You've done your homework."

"I talked to someone who mentioned you. Said you were investigating years ago, then stopped."

"I didn't stop." The woman's voice hardened. "I was stopped."

"What does that mean?"

The woman glanced around the garage, checking the shadows, the exits, the places where someone might be hiding. Then she reached into her coat and pulled out a manila envelope.

"My name is Vera Chen. Eight years ago, I was working on a story about wellness industry fraud. Financial irregularities, fake credentials, the usual stuff. Prana & Bones came up on my radar because of some inconsistencies in their nonprofit filings."

She held out the envelope. Celeste hesitated, then stepped forward to take it.

"I started digging," Vera continued. "Interviewed former employees, pulled public records, tried to get access to the principals. Maya Sharma agreed to talk to me. Very charming, very cooperative. Answered all my questions with that smile that makes you feel like you're the only person in the world."

"I've experienced that smile."

"Then you know. It's a weapon." Vera shoved her hands in her pockets. "I asked about her sister. About Mira. Said I wanted to interview both of them for the piece. Maya made excuses—Mira was traveling, Mira was private, Mira didn't do press. I pushed. I said I couldn't run the story without talking to both founders."

"What happened?"

"Maya's whole demeanor changed. Just for a second. Like a mask slipping. And then she smiled again and said, 'I'll see what I can do.'"

Vera's voice had gone flat, reciting facts like a police report.

"Three days later, I got a call from a woman who said she was Mira Sharma. Very different from Maya—softer voice, calmer energy. She agreed to meet me for coffee. I was excited. I thought I was about to crack the story open."

"Did you meet her?"

"I went to the coffee shop. I waited for two hours. She never showed." Vera paused. "But someone else did."

"Who?"

"I don't know. A man. Big, professional-looking. He sat down across from me and said, very calmly, that I should stop asking questions about Prana & Bones. He said that people who caused problems for the organization tended to have problems of their own. He said he knew where I lived, where my daughter went to school, what time my husband left for work in the morning."

Celeste felt ice spread through her chest. "He threatened your family?"

"He didn't threaten anything. He just stated facts. Addresses, schedules, routines. Things he couldn't have known unless he'd been watching us for weeks." Vera's jaw tightened. "Then he stood up and walked out. And that night, someone broke into my house while we were sleeping. Didn't take anything. Didn't hurt anyone. Just left a single shoe on my daughter's pillow."

"A shoe?"

"A left shoe. A child's sneaker. Not my daughter's—we'd never seen it before. But it was her size. Her favorite color."

Celeste's mind raced. The index cards. The jewelry. What else was being collected?

"I dropped the story," Vera said. "Moved my family to a different state. Tried to forget. But I kept tabs on Prana & Bones from a distance. Watched them grow. Watched Maya become a star. And watched other journalists start asking questions, then suddenly stop."

"How many?"

"At least four that I know of. A blogger in Seattle who was writing about cult-like practices in the wellness industry. A freelancer in Chicago who was investigating the disappearance of a retreat attendee. A podcaster in Austin who did an episode about red flags at Prana & Bones and then never mentioned them again."

"What happened to them?"

Vera shook her head slowly. "The blogger had a mental breakdown. Checked herself into a psychiatric facility, claimed she was being followed, being watched. Everyone thought she was paranoid. Maybe she was. The freelancer's investigation just... stopped. He wouldn't return my calls. The podcaster deleted the episode and all her social media, then moved to another country."

"And you think Prana & Bones was behind all of this?"

"I think someone connected to Prana & Bones has been systematically silencing anyone who gets too close to the truth." Vera nodded at the envelope in Celeste's hands. "That's everything I have. Property records, financial documents, interview transcripts. And something I found last year that I've never shown anyone."

Celeste opened the envelope and pulled out a stack of papers. Most of it looked like standard investigative material—public records, printed emails, handwritten notes. But at the bottom of the stack was a photograph.

Two women standing side by side. Same face, same dark hair, same high cheekbones. One had her hair pulled back in a sleek ponytail; the other wore hers loose around her shoulders. They were smiling at the camera, arms around each other, clearly sisters, clearly close.

"Where did you get this?" Celeste asked.

"Their mother."

"You talked to Sunita Sharma?"

"Once. Briefly. She was... not well. Very anxious, very paranoid. She kept saying she needed to tell someone the truth, but every time she started to explain, she'd stop herself. Say it wasn't safe. Say *she* might be listening."

"She?"

"I assumed she meant Maya. Or Mira. Or whoever." Vera pointed at the photograph. "She gave me that. Said it was the only photo of the two of them together. Said I should look at it closely. Said if I looked hard enough, I'd see."

"See what?"

"I don't know. I've stared at that photo for years. They look like sisters. They look like two separate people."

Celeste studied the image. Maya and Mira, side by side. Different clothes, different hair, different posture. But the same face. The exact same face.

Something nagged at her. Something about the photo that didn't quite—

"The shadow," she said suddenly.

"What?"

"Look at their shadows." Celeste tilted the photo toward the dim light of the parking garage. "They're standing right next to each other, but there's only one shadow."

Vera went still.

Celeste traced the outline with her finger. Both women were standing in sunlight, both at the same angle. But on the ground behind them, stretching across the pavement, there was only a single dark shape. One shadow for two bodies.

"That's not possible," Vera whispered. "That's—if they were both really there—"

"It's been doctored." Celeste's voice was flat. "Or they weren't both there. One of them was added later."

"But the mother gave me this. She said it was proof they were real."

"Maybe it's proof of something else." Celeste slipped the photo back into the envelope. "Maybe Sunita was trying to show you that something was wrong. That what you were seeing wasn't what you thought you were seeing."

They stood in silence for a long moment, the weight of the revelation settling over them like a shroud.

"There's one more thing," Vera said finally. "Something I didn't put in the envelope because I wasn't sure it was connected. But now…"

"What?"

"I tracked down one of the people from my original investigation. A woman who had attended a Prana & Bones retreat and then left suddenly, refused to talk about it. I found her three years ago. She was living in a group home in Nevada. Severe dissociative disorder. Couldn't hold a conversation for more than a few minutes before she'd start talking to people who weren't there."

Celeste felt her stomach drop. "What happened to her?"

"I don't know. But she kept saying the same thing, over and over. Said a woman had stolen something from her. Said she could feel the empty space where it used to be." Vera's voice was barely audible now. "She said, 'She breathed me in and I never came back out.'"

The wind picked up, whistling through the open sides of the garage. Celeste shivered despite herself.

"Ms. Park—Celeste—I came here tonight because I think you might actually be able to finish what I started. You have a personal stake. A reason to keep going even when it gets hard." Vera's eyes were intense, urgent. "But I need you to understand what you're dealing with. This isn't just fraud or bad business practices. There's something wrong with that woman. Something broken in a way that makes her dangerous."

"Which woman? Maya or Mira?"

Vera smiled grimly. "That's the question, isn't it? My honest answer? I don't think it matters. I don't think there's a difference."

A sound from the stairwell. Footsteps, echoing up through the concrete.

Both women froze.

"You should go," Vera said quickly. "Take the envelope. Don't contact me again—it's not safe for either of us. And Celeste?"

"Yes?"

"Your sister. Bree. I found her name in some of my old notes. She was one of the ones I was tracking—people who went to Prana & Bones and then... changed. Disappeared." Vera was backing toward her car now. "I don't know what happened to her. But if she got too close, if she saw something she wasn't supposed to see..."

The footsteps were getting louder. Closer.

"Find Sunita Sharma," Vera said. "The mother. She knows the truth. She's known it for decades. She's the only one who might be willing to tell you."

She got in her car, started the engine, and was gone before Celeste could respond.

The footsteps reached the top of the stairs.

Celeste's hand closed around the pepper spray in her pocket. She turned to face whoever was coming, heart hammering, envelope clutched to her chest.

A man emerged from the stairwell. Young, early twenties,

wearing earbuds and jogging clothes. He glanced at Celeste with vague surprise, nodded politely, and continued to a car on the other side of the level.

Just a runner. Just someone who'd parked here and was now leaving.

Celeste let out a breath she didn't know she'd been holding.

She looked down at the envelope in her hands. The photograph of two sisters with one shadow. The financial documents, the interview transcripts, the years of investigation that had led nowhere except to fear and silence.

And a name: Sunita Sharma. The mother who knew the truth.

Celeste walked to her car on legs that felt like they belonged to someone else. She got in, locked the doors, and sat in the darkness for a long time, staring at nothing.

She breathed me in and I never came back out.

What did that mean? What had Maya—or Mira—done to that woman in the group home? What had she done to all the people who'd gotten too close?

What had she done to Bree?

Celeste started the car and pulled out of the garage, merging into the late-night traffic with the envelope on the seat beside her and a new destination forming in her mind.

Sunita Sharma. The mother.

If anyone knew the truth, it was her.

And Celeste was going to find her.

12

Mira
The Unraveling

The woman in the mirror was cracking.

She could see it in the fine lines around her eyes, the tension in her jaw, the way her reflection seemed to flicker at the edges like a television losing signal. She had always been so careful about maintaining the surface—the smooth skin, the serene expression, the mask of calm that kept the world at bay. But the mask was slipping. She could feel it.

Three days since Maya had found the apartment.

Three days since everything began to fall apart.

She hadn't been there when Maya arrived—she'd been across town, handling a supplier meeting that couldn't be rescheduled. But she'd known the moment it happened. Had felt it like a physical sensation, a tearing somewhere deep in her chest. The walls she'd spent decades building, the careful architecture of separation and denial, all of it crumbling because Maya had finally done the one thing she was never supposed to do.

She had looked.

And now Maya wasn't answering her calls. Wasn't responding to texts. Had canceled all her classes for the rest of the week, citing a "family emergency." The studio was in chaos, students confused, staff scrambling to cover gaps in the schedule.

But worse than the practical problems was the silence.

Maya had always needed her. Had always called, texted, reached out for reassurance and guidance and the steady hand that kept her from flying apart. That neediness had been exhausting sometimes, but it had also been useful. It had kept Maya dependent. Controllable. Safe.

Now there was nothing. Just a void where her sister used to be.

She's not your sister, a voice whispered in the back of her mind. *She never was. She's you. A piece of you that you cut away and pretended was someone else.*

She pushed the voice down. She was good at pushing things down.

The apartment felt different now. Contaminated. Maya had been here, had touched her things, had opened the boxes and seen what was inside. The space that had always felt like a sanctuary—the one place where she could be fully herself without performance or pretense—now felt exposed. Violated.

She should move the collection. She knew that. Should find a new hiding place, a storage unit somewhere, a safety deposit box. But the thought of touching those objects right now, of handling the jewelry and the cards and the shoes, made her skin crawl. They felt tainted somehow. Seen.

Her phone buzzed. Not Maya—she checked every time, hoping despite herself—but K.

Update on C.P.?

She stared at the message for a long moment. Celeste Park. The journalist. In all the chaos of the past few days, she'd almost forgotten about that particular problem. But problems didn't go away just because you ignored them. Problems grew. Problems metastasized.

She typed back: *Met with someone last night. Parking garage on 38th. Couldn't get close enough to hear.*

The response came immediately: *Who?*

Unknown. Older woman. Dark sedan. They talked for approximately 15 minutes, then the woman left. C.P. stayed in her car for another 20 minutes before driving home.

Did C.P. receive anything?

She hesitated. She'd watched from four levels down, using binoculars she'd bought specifically for this purpose. The distance and the darkness had made details difficult, but she'd seen the envelope pass between them. Had seen Celeste clutch it to her chest like something precious.

Yes. A manila envelope. Unknown contents.

A longer pause this time. Then: *This is escalating. We need to consider more direct intervention.*

Define direct.

The kind that ends the problem permanently.

She set the phone down and walked to the window. The city sprawled below her, millions of lives intersecting and diverging, people going about their business with no idea what moved among them. What watched. What waited.

She had never killed anyone.

That was important to remember. Important to hold onto. She had destroyed careers, yes. Had driven people away, had silenced threats, had made problems disappear through careful application of pressure and fear. But she had never crossed that final line. Had never taken a life with her own hands.

Your hands, the voice whispered again. *Maya's hands. The same hands.*

She pressed her palms against the cold glass of the window and watched her breath fog the surface.

The journalist was getting too close. The meeting in the parking garage proved it—Celeste had found others, was building a network, was accumulating evidence that couldn't be explained away or buried. And somewhere in that manila envelope was information that could unravel everything.

She should be afraid. A normal person would be afraid.

Instead, she felt something else. Something that uncurled in her chest like a sleeping animal waking up. Something that looked at the growing threat and saw not danger but opportunity.

Let her come, the feeling whispered. *Let her dig. Let her find all the pieces and put them together. And when she thinks she understands, when she thinks she's won—*

Show her what she's really dealing with.

Her phone buzzed again. K: *Are you still there?*

She picked up the phone and typed: *I'll handle it.*

How?

My way.

She didn't wait for a response. Instead, she pulled up Celeste's information—the address she'd obtained weeks ago, the phone number, the license plate, the daily schedule she'd been tracking since the interview.

Celeste lived alone in a small apartment in Brooklyn. She worked from home most days, went to the *Wellspring* office on Tuesdays and Thursdays, frequented a coffee shop on the corner of her block. She jogged in the mornings when the weather was good. She ordered takeout at least four times a week—Thai, mostly, from a place called Siam Garden.

She was predictable. Vulnerable. Alone.

Just like Bree had been.

The thought surfaced before she could stop it, bringing with it a cascade of memories she usually kept locked away. Bree at the retreat, eyes shining with desperate hope. Bree in the sharing circles, spilling her trauma like an offering. Bree following Maya around like a lost puppy, convinced that someone finally understood her.

Bree had been a problem. Not immediately—at first she'd been useful, a devoted student who brought energy and enthusiasm to every class. But then she'd started wanting more. Started showing up at the studio unannounced, sending long emails at 3 AM, talking about moving to be closer to "her teachers."

The neediness had been suffocating. The attachment had been dangerous. And when Bree started asking questions—about Maya's past, about the discrepancies in her story, about the sister she could never seem to meet in person—she had become a liability.

So she had been handled.

Not killed. Never killed. Just... redirected. A suggestion about an ashram in Thailand, a glowing recommendation, a gentle push toward a path that led far away from Prana & Bones. Bree had gone willingly, even eagerly, convinced that she was embarking on the next stage of her spiritual journey.

What happened after that wasn't her responsibility. If Bree had wandered into trouble in a foreign country, if she'd joined some more dangerous organization, if she'd simply decided to disappear—those were choices Bree had made. Not her. Never her.

But you knew, the voice whispered. *You knew she was fragile. You knew she wouldn't survive alone. You sent her away knowing she might never come back.*

She shook her head, physically trying to dislodge the thought. This was pointless. Bree was gone—had been gone for years. What mattered now was Celeste.

What mattered was survival.

She pulled on her coat and grabbed her keys. The studio was quiet at this hour—late evening, between the after-work rush and the night classes. A good time to be alone. A good time to think.

But when she arrived, the studio wasn't empty.

Devi was still there, finishing some administrative work at the front desk. She looked up when the door opened, and her face did something complicated—surprise, confusion, a flicker of something that might have been fear.

"Maya? I thought you were—are you feeling better?"

She froze for just a moment. She was dressed as Mira tonight—hair down, soft clothes, silver rings. But Devi had clearly expected Maya. Had clearly thought—

"It's Mira," she said smoothly. "Maya's still resting. I came to check on a few things."

"Oh." Devi's face relaxed slightly, but the confusion remained. "Of course. I just—for a second, I thought—never mind. Is there anything you need?"

"Just some quiet time. You can head home."

"Are you sure? I don't mind staying—"

"I'm sure." The words came out sharper than intended. She softened her voice, forced the Mira-warmth back into it. "Thank you, Devi. You work so hard. Go home. Rest."

Devi nodded, gathered her things, and left with one last uncertain glance over her shoulder.

Alone at last.

She moved through the studio slowly, touching things, remembering. The bamboo floors she'd selected herself. The altar with its singing bowls and crystals and bronze Shiva. The windows that looked out over the city, the same windows Maya had stood at during her interview with Celeste.

This was what she was protecting. This empire they'd built

together—or rather, that she had built while Maya took the credit. Every brick, every student, every dollar had passed through her hands at some point. She had created this. She had earned it.

And she would not let some journalist with a dead sister take it away.

The evening class was starting in an hour. Yin yoga. Her class—Mira's class. She hadn't planned to teach tonight, but suddenly she needed it. Needed the routine, the control, the power of standing in front of a room full of people who trusted her completely.

She changed into her teaching clothes and began preparing the room. Bolsters against the wall. Blankets in perfect thirds. Eye pillows lined up like sleeping birds.

Students began arriving. The woman with sad eyes—she'd become a regular. The young man who couldn't sleep. New faces mixed with familiar ones, all of them seeking something, all of them hoping she could provide it.

"Welcome," she said, her voice dropping into that lower register that made people feel safe. "Find a comfortable seat. Let your eyes close if that feels safe. And just begin to notice your breath."

She watched them sink into themselves. Watched the tension drain from their shoulders, the masks slip from their faces. They were so open. So trusting. So completely at her mercy.

The class proceeded normally through the first three poses. Supported child's pose. Reclined twist. Caterpillar, folding forward over extended legs.

And then, during the fourth pose—a long-held hip opener that always brought up emotions—she felt it.

The hunger.

It had been building for days. Maybe weeks. The stress of

the journalist, the crisis with Maya, the constant vigilance required to keep everything from falling apart. She'd been so focused on damage control that she'd neglected her own needs.

Now those needs announced themselves with sudden, desperate intensity.

She moved through the room during the hold, adjusting students, offering gentle touches. But her attention was fixed on one woman in particular.

New student. Late twenties. Beautiful in a fragile way, with dark circles under her eyes and a tremor in her hands that suggested she hadn't been sleeping. She'd introduced herself before class as Mariana, had mentioned that she was going through a divorce, that a friend had recommended Prana & Bones as a place to heal.

Vulnerable. Desperate. Perfect.

She made her way to Mariana's mat. Knelt down beside her. Placed one hand on her lower back and one on her shoulder—a standard adjustment, nothing unusual.

"Breathe here," she murmured. "Let yourself feel whatever comes up."

Mariana made a small sound. Her body softened under the touch.

And something in Mira softened too—but in a different way. In the way a predator softens before the strike.

She leaned closer. Close enough to smell the lavender of Mariana's shampoo, the salt of old tears still clinging to her skin. Close enough to feel the warmth radiating off her body.

Close enough to breathe.

She inhaled slowly, silently. Drew in the air that Mariana was exhaling. Felt it fill her lungs—not just oxygen, but something else. Something she had no name for but had learned to recognize. The essence of another person's surrender.

Mariana shuddered beneath her hands. "That feels..." She trailed off, unable to find the words.

"I know," Mira whispered. "Let it go. I've got you."

She held the breath for a long moment. Felt the stolen warmth spread through her chest, filling spaces she hadn't realized were empty. Then she exhaled slowly and moved on to the next student.

Mariana stayed in the pose for another five minutes, tears streaming silently down her cheeks.

By the end of class, Mira felt almost normal again. Almost calm. The hunger had been fed—not fully, never fully, but enough to take the edge off. Enough to think clearly.

As students rolled up their mats and gathered their things, she noticed something.

Mariana had left her shoes by the door. Simple leather sandals, the left one slightly askew.

She glanced around. Mariana was in the bathroom, probably splashing water on her tear-stained face. The other students were occupied with their own departures.

No one was watching.

She shouldn't. It was too risky, too soon after Maya's discovery. The collection was already compromised. Adding to it now would be reckless.

But the hunger had its own logic. Its own needs.

Her hand moved before she could stop it. Picked up the left sandal. Slipped it into her bag.

By the time Mariana emerged from the bathroom, confused about her missing shoe, Mira was already gone.

Back in her apartment, she sat on the floor of her closet, the sandal in her lap.

She should throw it away. Should get rid of all of it—the

jewelry, the cards, the trunk full of shoes. Should burn it all and start fresh, unburdened by evidence.

But she couldn't.

These were her proof. Her trophies. Her collection of captured moments, each object representing a person who had given themselves to her completely, even if they didn't know it.

She opened the cedar chest and looked at the shoes inside. Decades of acquisitions, organized by date. The oldest ones were nearly falling apart—cheap sneakers from her first yoga classes, back when she was just learning what she could take from people and how.

The newest ones were from the past year. A designer heel from a wealthy donor. A running shoe from a fitness influencer who'd attended a retreat. A child's Mary Jane from—

She stopped.

The child's shoe. She didn't remember taking it.

She picked it up carefully, examining it in the dim light. Pink patent leather with a small strap. Size 3. No tag, no date, no memory of acquisition.

When had she taken this? From whom?

A flash of something—not quite memory, more like the shadow of one. A school pickup line. A mother distracted by her phone. A small pink shoe left momentarily unattended.

But she didn't take children's shoes. That was a rule. She had rules about these things. Children were off-limits. Children were innocent.

Are they? the voice asked. *Or do they just remind you of yourself? Of the child you used to be, before everything broke?*

She dropped the shoe back into the trunk and slammed the lid closed.

This was wrong. Something was wrong. The rules were important. The rules kept her safe, kept her controlled, kept her from becoming something worse than she already was.

But the rules were eroding. She could feel it—the boundaries she'd maintained for years growing soft and porous, letting things through that should have stayed locked away.

Maya's discovery had destabilized everything. Not just practically, but psychologically. The walls between them were thinner now. The separation was failing.

And something else was emerging. Something older. Something that had been waiting in the darkness for a very long time.

She pressed her hands against her temples and tried to breathe.

Stay in control. Stay calm. Handle the journalist. Handle Maya. Handle everything, the way you always have.

But for the first time in years, she wasn't sure she could.

For the first time in years, she wasn't sure who was in control at all.

Her phone buzzed. A text from an unknown number.

I know what you are.

She stared at the screen, heart pounding.

Another message appeared: *The mother told me everything.*

And then, a third: *You can't make me disappear like the others.*

No signature. No identification. But she knew who it was.

Celeste Park.

The journalist had found Sunita. Had heard the truth. And now she was making her move.

The game had changed. The hunter was becoming the hunted.

And somewhere in the darkness of her mind, something that was neither Maya nor Mira opened its eyes and began to smile.

13

Maya
The Voicemail
Four days since the apartment.
Maya hadn't left her bed in three of them.

She lay in the darkness of her bedroom, curtains drawn against the daylight, phone turned off, the world reduced to the small cocoon of blankets and silence she'd constructed around herself. She didn't eat. She barely drank. She slept in fits and starts, haunted by dreams she couldn't remember but woke from gasping, her hands clutching at her throat as if trying to stop something from escaping.

Or trying to stop something from getting in.

The boxes haunted her. Even with her eyes closed, she could see them—the velvet jewelry case, the wooden box of index cards, the cedar chest full of single left shoes. She could see the handwriting on the tags, so familiar, so undeniably her own. She could see the card that had broken her:

Maya S. — created to carry the softness. Doesn't know she's not real.

Created. Like a character in a story. Like a mask someone puts on and takes off at will.

She wasn't real. She had never been real. Everything she thought she knew about herself—her history, her personality, her relationships—was a fiction. A comfortable lie told by some deeper, darker self that used her as a costume.

No, a voice whispered in the back of her mind. *That's not right. You're real. You're the one who's always been here. The other one is the fiction.*

But how could she know? How could she trust any of her memories, any of her perceptions, when her own mind had been lying to her for decades?

She thought about her mother's voicemail. *Those are your hands, Maya. They've always been your hands.*

She thought about Mira's phone calls, all those years of conversations with a sister who might never have existed outside her own fractured consciousness.

She thought about the students—the names on those index cards, the jewelry in that velvet box, the shoes in that cedar chest. How many people had she touched, had she stolen from, had she *handled* without ever knowing it?

Handled permanently.

What did that mean? What had her hands done while she wasn't watching?

A sound penetrated the fog of her thoughts. Her phone—she'd turned it back on at some point, though she didn't remember doing so. It was buzzing insistently on the nightstand, the screen lighting up with notifications she'd been ignoring for days.

Voicemails. Dozens of them. From the studio, from her publicist, from students and staff and people whose names she couldn't place. And mixed among them, calls from a number she didn't recognize.

She should ignore it. Should turn the phone off again and sink back into the darkness where nothing could reach her.

Instead, she picked it up.

The most recent voicemail was from ten minutes ago. Unknown number. She pressed play before she could talk herself out of it.

Her own voice filled the room.

But not her voice—not the voice she heard when she spoke, not the warm and welcoming tone she used to greet students. This voice was colder. Flatter. Each word precisely placed, like stones being laid in a wall.

"Maya. I know you're listening. I know you found the apartment. I know you saw what's in those boxes, and I know you're lying in bed right now trying to convince yourself that none of it is real."

Maya's hand trembled. She nearly dropped the phone.

"But it is real. All of it. The jewelry, the cards, the shoes—those are real. The people whose names are on those tags—they're real too. Or they were."

A pause. When the voice continued, there was something almost like tenderness in it.

"You think you're the victim here. You think you're the innocent one, the one who was lied to and manipulated. But Maya, sweetheart, you have to understand—you're not innocent. You never were. You're just the part that gets to forget."

Maya pressed her free hand over her mouth, trying to hold in the sob that was building in her chest.

"I'm not your enemy. I'm not even separate from you—not really. I'm just the part of you that does what needs to be done. The part that handles things. The part that survives." The voice softened further. "I've been protecting you your whole life. Every problem you never had to face, every threat that disappeared before you knew it existed, every morning you woke up with clean hands and a clear conscience—that was me. That was us. Working together, even if you didn't know it."

A longer pause. When the voice returned, the tenderness was gone.

"But things have changed. The journalist is getting too close. She's found the mother. She knows things that can't be unknown. And if she keeps digging—if she puts all the pieces together and goes public—everything we've built will be destroyed."

Maya realized she was holding her breath.

"I need you to understand something, Maya. I need you to really hear this." The voice dropped to barely above a whisper. "I will do whatever it takes to protect us. Whatever it takes. And if you try to stop me—if you go to the police, or talk to the journalist, or do anything to interfere with what needs to happen— I will handle you the same way I've handled everyone else."

Silence.

Then, almost gently: "I don't want to. You're the best part of me—the part that can still feel things, still connect with people, still believe the world is good. Losing you would be like losing a limb. But I'll do it if I have to. I'll do it to survive."

Another pause.

"Go back to sleep, Maya. Let me handle this. It's what I was made for."

The voicemail ended.

Maya sat frozen in the darkness, the phone still pressed to her ear, listening to nothing.

It's what I was made for.

Made. Mira had said she was *made*. But the index card—the one about Maya—had said Maya was the created one. The one who didn't know she was not real.

So which of them was the original? Which of them had made the other?

Or had they both been made by something else entirely?

Her phone buzzed. A new voicemail. Same unknown number.

She shouldn't listen. She should throw the phone across the room, should run out of this apartment and never come back, should find a hospital and check herself in and beg someone to help her understand what she was.

Her finger pressed play.

The voice was different this time. Not the cold, flat voice from before. Not Mira. This voice was younger, higher, with a strange, hollow quality—like an echo in an empty room.

"She's wrong, you know. Mira. She thinks she's the strong one. She thinks she made you." A pause. "But Mira doesn't remember. Mira can't remember, because I made her not to."

Maya's blood went cold.

"I'm the one who found the papers. I'm the one who read the birth certificate and the death certificate and learned that there was supposed to be two of us." The voice wavered slightly. "Two of us, Maya. We were supposed to be twins. But she died. Two days old and she just... stopped."

Something cracked in Maya's chest. A fault line she hadn't known existed.

"I couldn't stand it. Being half of something that was supposed to be whole. So I made her. I gave her a name—Mira, because it sounds like mirror, because that's what she was supposed to be. My mirror. My other half."

The voice grew quieter, more distant.

"But I made her wrong. Or maybe she grew wrong. I meant for her to be soft, like I imagined my sister would have been. Someone to talk to. Someone to share things with. But she became something else. Something hard. Something that takes and takes and never feels full."

A long silence. When the voice returned, it was barely audible.

"And then I couldn't carry it anymore. The knowing. The grief. The weight of what I'd done. So I made another one. I made you, Maya. The bright one. The one who gets to feel things without remembering why."

Maya was crying now. Silent tears streaming down her face.

"You're not the original. Neither is Mira. I am. I'm what's left of the girl who found those papers when she was nine years old and broke into so many pieces she doesn't even have a name anymore."

The voice cracked.

"The journalist is close. She's talked to Mom. She's going to find out about the twin—the real one, the one who died. And when she does, she's going to understand what we really are."

"Not a person. Not even two people. Just a collection of fragments, held together by grief and pretending to be whole."

A final pause.

"I'm tired, Maya. I've been holding us together for so long. And I don't think I can do it anymore."

The voicemail ended.

Maya sat in the darkness, the phone slipping from her nerveless fingers, and felt the architecture of her self begin to collapse.

A twin. She'd had a twin who died. And the grief of that loss—a loss she didn't even consciously remember—had shattered her into pieces.

Mira wasn't her sister. Mira was a ghost she'd created to fill the space where her real sister should have been.

And Maya herself—the Maya who taught classes and gave interviews and believed she was a whole, complete person—was just another fragment. Another mask. Another way of not facing the unbearable truth.

She wasn't one person pretending to be two.

She was no one pretending to be someone.

And the original—the nine-year-old who had broken under the weight of a grief she couldn't name—was still in there somewhere. Still carrying all of it. Still falling apart.

Maya curled into a ball on her bed and let the tears come.

She didn't know who she was anymore. Didn't know what was real and what was invention. Didn't know how to exist in a world where the ground beneath her feet had turned out to be nothing but air.

But somewhere in the depths of her fractured mind, a small voice whispered:

You have to find Mom. You have to know the truth. All of it.

Before Mira handles that too.

14

Celeste
The Records

The documents spread across Celeste's kitchen table like evidence at a crime scene.

Property records. Bank statements. Business filings. Tax returns. Every piece of paper she'd accumulated over the past two weeks, plus everything from Vera Chen's envelope, laid out in careful rows and columns as she tried to make sense of what she was seeing.

The story the documents told was impossible. And yet.

She picked up the property deed for Mira's apartment—the brownstone in Brooklyn, apartment 3B. The owner was listed clearly, in black and white: Maya Sharma. Not Mira. Maya.

She picked up the lease agreement for the Prana & Bones flagship studio. Signed by Maya Sharma. No co-signer. No mention of Mira.

The business registration for Prana & Bones LLC. Filed by Maya Sharma, sole proprietor.

The bank accounts—operating, payroll, savings. All in Maya's name. All with Maya's signature. Every check, every wire transfer, every financial transaction for the past twelve years, authorized by one person.

And only one person.

There was no Mira.

Not on any deed. Not on any license. Not on any bank account or tax return or legal document of any kind. Mira Sharma, co-founder of Prana & Bones, the quiet sister who handled the business side while Maya handled the spotlight, did not exist on paper.

She existed in photographs—Celeste had seen them. She existed in class schedules and staff memories and student testimonials. She existed in the soft voice on the yoga nidra recordings and the silver rings that glinted in the candlelight.

But legally, officially, on paper?

Mira Sharma was a ghost.

Celeste sat back in her chair and rubbed her eyes. It was after midnight. She'd been staring at these documents for hours, checking and rechecking, sure she must be missing something. A second signature hidden somewhere. A power of attorney. A business partner agreement. Something, anything, that would prove Mira was a separate person and not—

Not what? What was the alternative?

She thought about Jonah Whitfield's words in the coffee shop. *I don't think there are two of them. I don't think there ever were.*

She thought about Vera Chen in the parking garage. *I don't think it matters. I don't think there's a difference.*

She thought about the photograph with one shadow.

And she thought about what Sunita Sharma had told her two days ago, in a conversation that still made her chest ache with a strange, unexpected grief.

. . .

Finding Maya's mother had been easier than expected.

Sunita Sharma lived in a small house in New Jersey, just across the river from the city but a world away from the gleaming studios and wellness empire her daughter had built. The house was modest, well-maintained, with a garden out front that was going slightly wild—the kind of garden that belonged to someone who had once cared very much and now cared less.

Celeste had knocked on the door at 10 AM on a Tuesday, not sure what to expect. The woman who answered was small, gray-haired, with eyes that held decades of exhaustion—and something else. Something that looked like relief.

"Mrs. Sharma? My name is Celeste Park. I'm a journalist, and I'm writing about Prana & Bones. I was hoping—"

"I know who you are."

The words stopped Celeste cold.

"You're the one who's been asking questions. The one with the sister who disappeared." Sunita's voice was soft, almost gentle. "I wondered when you would find me."

"May I come in?"

Sunita studied her for a long moment. Her eyes were wet, but she didn't look away.

"Yes," she said finally. "I think it's time."

The house was cluttered in a way that suggested accumulated grief—stacks of magazines that hadn't been read, mail that hadn't been opened, photographs in frames that were dusty with neglect. But on every surface, in every room, there were images of the same face: a dark-haired girl at various ages, smiling, dancing, blowing out birthday candles.

Only one girl. Never two.

Sunita led her to a small living room and gestured to a worn couch.

"Tea?"

"No, thank you. I just have some questions—"

"I know what questions you have." Sunita sat across from her in an armchair that had molded itself to her body over years of use. "You want to know about Mira."

Celeste nodded.

"You haven't been able to find any documentation of her existence. No property records, no business filings, nothing. And no one you've talked to can remember seeing her and Maya in the same room at the same time."

"That's right."

Sunita was quiet for a long moment. Her hands twisted in her lap—once, twice, three times—before she spoke.

"There's a reason for that." She looked up at Celeste with eyes that had seen too much. "Mira doesn't exist. She never has. Not the way you think."

Celeste felt her heart rate spike, but she kept her voice steady. "What do you mean?"

"I mean that Mira Sharma died thirty-four years ago. Two days after she was born."

The room seemed to contract around Celeste.

"Maya was a twin," Sunita continued, her voice barely above a whisper. "Identical. They were born two minutes apart—Maya first, then Mira. But Mira was smaller. Weaker. Her lungs weren't fully developed." She pressed her hand to her chest, as if feeling an old wound. "She lived for forty-eight hours. And then she was gone."

"Maya had a twin sister who died."

"Yes."

"And you never told her?"

Sunita's face crumpled. "How could I? She was so young. So happy. I thought—I thought if she didn't know, she wouldn't have to grieve. I thought I was protecting her." She shook her head slowly. "I kept the documents. The birth certificates, the death certificate, the hospital bracelet. I couldn't throw them away—it felt like throwing away my daughter. So I hid them in a box in my closet and tried to forget."

"But Maya found them."

"When she was nine." Sunita's voice cracked. "I came home from work and she was sitting on my bedroom floor, surrounded by papers, holding that tiny hospital bracelet in her hands. She looked up at me and said, 'Mommy, why didn't you tell me I had a sister?'"

Celeste felt something twist in her chest. A nine-year-old girl, discovering that she'd been half of something and never known it.

"What happened after that?"

"At first, nothing obvious. She was sad, withdrawn. She asked a lot of questions about Mira—what she looked like, what the doctors said, whether she suffered. I answered as best I could." Sunita wiped her eyes with the back of her hand. "And then, about a week later, she started talking about Mira in the present tense."

"Present tense?"

"'Mira thinks this.' 'Mira wants that.' 'Mira says I shouldn't be sad anymore because she's not really gone.'" Sunita's voice had gone distant, reciting memories worn smooth by repetition. "I thought it was a phase. A coping mechanism. The therapist said imaginary companions were common for children processing grief, that she'd grow out of it."

"But she didn't."

"No. She grew into it." Sunita looked at Celeste with haunted eyes. "The imaginary friend became a voice. The voice became a presence. The presence became... something else. Something that didn't just live in Maya's imagination but took over her body sometimes. Changed the way she talked, the way she moved, the way she looked at people."

"Dissociative identity disorder."

Sunita nodded. "That's what the doctors called it, eventually. Years later, after I'd taken her to specialist after specialist, after I'd watched my daughter split into pieces and couldn't do anything to stop it. DID. A fragmentation of identity, usually caused by severe childhood trauma." She laughed bitterly. "They asked what trauma Maya had experienced. I had to tell them: the trauma was learning she was supposed to be a twin. The trauma was finding out she'd been half of something and hadn't known."

"And Mira—the alter, the other personality—she took on the identity of the dead sister?"

"Yes and no." Sunita stood abruptly and walked to a bookshelf. She pulled out a small wooden box and brought it back to her chair. "Maya created Mira to fill the emptiness. To be the sister she should have had. But what she created wasn't... wasn't soft, the way Maya imagined her twin would have been."

She opened the box and pulled out a folded piece of paper, yellowed with age.

"I found this in Maya's room when she was ten. A year after she discovered the truth."

She handed it to Celeste.

The paper was notebook paper, torn from a spiral binding. The handwriting was a child's—uneven, oversized, letters that hadn't yet learned to stay between the lines.

Dear Mira,

Today I found out you were real. Mom doesn't know I found the papers in her closet. I'm not supposed to know about you. But now I do.

I always felt like something was missing. Like there was supposed to be someone else. Now I know why.

You were supposed to be here with me. We were supposed to do everything together. But you died and I didn't and that's not fair. That's not fair that's not fair that's NOT FAIR.

So I decided. You're not dead anymore. I'm going to keep you alive. I'm going to talk to you and think about you and make a place for you inside me where you can live.

You can have half of everything. Half my room, half my toys, half my thoughts. Half of me.

I won't be alone anymore. And you won't be dead.

Love, Maya (age 9)

Celeste read the letter twice. Her hands were shaking slightly when she set it down.

"She created her," Celeste said quietly. "Out of grief. Out of loneliness."

"Yes." Sunita took the letter back, handling it gently, like something precious and terrible. "But what she created wasn't the soft, sweet sister she imagined. The Mira who emerged was... harder. Colder. She was the part of Maya that could handle things. The part that didn't feel pain, didn't feel guilt, didn't feel anything except the need to survive."

"And Maya? The Maya who exists now?"

"Another fragment." Sunita returned the letter to the box and closed the lid. "When the weight of what she'd done—creating this other self, letting it grow, losing control of it—became too much, Maya split again. She created a new version of herself. A softer version. One that didn't remember the grief, didn't remember the choice, didn't know she wasn't the original."

"So there are three of them."

Sunita shook her head slowly. "There were three. The original Maya—the one who found the papers and made the choice—she retreated a long time ago. Went so deep inside that even Mira can't always reach her. What's left is Maya and Mira: the face and the hands. The one who feels and the one who acts.

The one the world loves and the one who does whatever it takes to protect her."

"Protect her how?"

Sunita's face went very still.

"There have been... incidents. Over the years. People who got too close. People who asked too many questions. People who threatened to expose the truth about Maya's condition." She paused. "They tend to go away."

"Go away how?"

"Some of them had breakdowns. Psychiatric episodes that discredited them. Some of them simply disappeared—moved away, changed their names, stopped contacting anyone they used to know." Sunita's voice dropped. "And some of them... I don't know what happened to them. But I have my suspicions."

"You think Mira killed them?"

The word hung between them—sharp, brutal, unavoidable.

"I think Mira handles problems," Sunita said carefully. "And I think some problems can only be handled one way."

Celeste thought about Bree. About the retreat in Tulum, the gradual estrangement, the final silence.

"My sister," she said. "Bree. She attended a Prana & Bones retreat four years ago. She came back different. And then she disappeared."

Sunita's eyes filled with tears. "I know. I saw her name in Mira's notes once. I know what they wrote about her." She reached out and took Celeste's hand. "I'm so sorry. I'm so sorry for what my daughter has become. For what I helped create by keeping secrets I should have told."

"What did the notes say?"

"That she was a risk. That she was too attached, too unstable, too likely to cause problems." Sunita squeezed her hand. "That she needed to be redirected."

"Redirected where?"

"An ashram. Somewhere overseas. Thailand or India—I don't remember." Sunita's voice was barely audible. "But I don't think she ever arrived. I don't think any of the redirected ones arrive where they're supposed to go."

Celeste pulled her hand away. She felt cold all over, despite the warmth of the room.

"Why are you telling me this? Why now?"

"Because you're the first person who's gotten this close without being destroyed yet. Because you have a reason to keep going that the others didn't have." Sunita leaned forward, her eyes intense despite the tears. "And because something has changed. Something is different this time."

"Different how?"

"Maya is waking up. The real Maya—not the soft one, not the fragment. The original. The one who made Mira in the first place." Sunita's voice trembled. "I can feel it. After thirty-four years of sleep, she's starting to surface. And I don't know what happens when she does."

"What do you think happens?"

Sunita was quiet for a long moment.

"Mira exists because Maya couldn't bear to be alone. She was created from grief, from loneliness, from a child's desperate need to fill an impossible void." She looked at Celeste with something like fear in her eyes. "But grief doesn't stay soft forever. Loneliness doesn't stay gentle. The void Maya was trying to fill—it's been growing for thirty-four years. And Mira has been feeding it."

"Feeding it how?"

"With pieces of people. Their jewelry, their hair, their breath. Little fragments she takes without them knowing." Sunita shook her head. "And when that's not enough—when the void demands more—she takes bigger pieces. She takes their lives, their sanity, their ability to threaten what Maya has built."

"And the original Maya? The one who's waking up?"

"She's been carrying all of it. The grief, the guilt, the weight of everything Mira has done in her name. For thirty-four years, she's been buried under it all, too broken to surface." Sunita's voice cracked. "But something has cracked the walls. Something has let her start to climb out. And when she emerges—when she sees what her creation has become—"

She didn't finish the sentence.

She didn't have to.

Celeste left Sunita's house with her head spinning and her chest aching with a grief that wasn't entirely her own.

A nine-year-old girl, finding out she was supposed to be a twin. Writing a letter to a dead sister, promising to keep her alive. Making a place inside herself for someone who had never really existed.

And that place had grown teeth.

She drove home in silence, the documents from Vera Chen and the story from Sunita swirling together in her mind. By the time she reached her apartment, she knew what she had to do.

She spread the documents across her kitchen table. Property records, bank statements, business filings. All of them pointing to the same impossible truth.

There was no Mira Sharma. There never had been.

There was only Maya—fractured, multiple, haunted by a grief she'd never been allowed to process. A woman who had split herself into pieces to survive an unbearable loss, and whose pieces had grown into something monstrous.

Celeste pulled out her laptop and opened a new document.

Her fingers hovered over the keys.

She thought about Bree. About the sister she'd lost, the

sister she'd been searching for, the sister who had probably been *handled* by a woman who didn't even know she was doing it.

She thought about Sunita, trapped for thirty-four years with a daughter she couldn't save.

She thought about Maya—the soft one, the fragment, the face the world loved—and wondered if there was anything left of her worth saving.

And she thought about the original. The nine-year-old who had made a choice out of grief and loneliness and had been buried under its consequences ever since.

What happened when that child finally woke up?

What happened when she saw what she had become?

Celeste began to type.

THE TRUTH ABOUT PRANA & BONES *By Celeste Park*

Maya Sharma is not who she appears to be.

The charismatic yoga guru and wellness entrepreneur has been hiding a secret for over thirty years—a secret that has left a trail of broken lives, disappeared people, and unanswered questions.

Documents obtained by this reporter reveal that Mira Sharma, the supposed co-founder of Prana & Bones and Maya's reclusive sister, does not exist. Not on paper. Not legally. Not anywhere except in the carefully constructed mythology of Maya's public persona.

But the deception goes far deeper than a phantom business partner.

Because Mira Sharma did exist once. She was Maya's identical twin, born two minutes after her on a spring morning thirty-four years ago.

She died forty-eight hours later.

And Maya has been keeping her alive ever since.

. . .

She wrote until the sun came up.

She wrote about the twin who died and the child who couldn't let go. She wrote about the documents in a closet and the letter from a nine-year-old promising to share half of everything with a sister who was already gone. She wrote about the fragmentation, the alter who grew harder and colder over the years, the people who had been *handled* when they got too close.

She wrote about Bree.

By the time she finished, she had fifteen thousand words. A first draft—rough, incomplete, but enough. Enough to take to her editor. Enough to go public.

Enough to expose what Maya Sharma really was.

She saved the document three times—laptop, external drive, cloud account. Emailed it to herself and to two trusted contacts with instructions to publish if anything happened to her.

Then she picked up her phone and composed a text to the unknown number that had been watching her:

I know what Maya is. I know about the twin. I'm going public.

She hit send.

The response came in under a minute:

You don't know as much as you think you do. But you're about to learn.

Before she could respond, another message appeared:

Check your door.

Her blood went cold.

She walked to her apartment door on legs that didn't feel like her own. Pressed her eye to the peephole.

Empty hallway.

She unlocked the door and opened it a crack.

On the worn carpet, directly in front of her threshold, sat a single object.

A shoe.

A left shoe. White canvas sneaker, low-top, with a faded rainbow stripe across the side. The kind they sold at Target for twenty dollars—nothing special, nothing expensive, the kind of shoe a million women owned.

Celeste's legs gave out. She grabbed the doorframe to keep from falling.

She knew that shoe.

The morning of Bree's flight to Tulum, they'd had breakfast together at Celeste's apartment. Celeste had been skeptical of the retreat—had made too many comments about "wellness cults" and "expensive navel-gazing"—and Bree had been defensive, and the meal had been tense in that particular way of sisters who love each other but can't stop picking at old wounds.

And then Celeste had knocked over her coffee.

The mug had tipped, and the coffee had splashed across the table and onto Bree's shoe—her left shoe, the one she'd propped on the edge of her chair the way she always did, the way their mother had always told her not to.

Bree had yelped. Celeste had grabbed napkins, apologizing frantically, dabbing at the brown stain spreading across the white canvas. But it wouldn't come out. The coffee had soaked into the fabric, leaving an ugly rust-colored blotch on the toe.

"Great," Bree had said, but she was laughing despite herself. "Now I'll be the girl with the coffee shoe. Very zen. Very spiritual retreat energy. They'll probably make me do extra meditation for showing up looking like a slob."

"Hold on." Celeste had rummaged through her junk drawer and pulled out a silver Sharpie. "Hold still."

She'd knelt on the kitchen floor and taken Bree's foot in her hands. And carefully, slowly, she'd drawn a tiny cartoon coffee cup around the stain—a little mug with a curling wisp of steam rising from it, transforming the accident into something intentional.

Bree had looked at it and burst out laughing. "You're such a dork."

"Now it's art," Celeste had said. "You're welcome."

An hour later, she'd driven Bree to the airport. Had taken the photograph that would become her obsession—Bree grinning under the weight of her overstuffed backpack, one hand raised in a wave, wearing cutoff shorts and a tank top and those white canvas sneakers with the rainbow stripe.

The left shoe with the tiny silver coffee cup on the toe.

Celeste had described that shoe a hundred times. To ashram administrators in Thailand who listened politely and promised to check their records. To hostel managers in India who shook their heads and said they'd never seen anyone matching that description. To police officers in three different countries who took notes they would never follow up on, their eyes glazing over as she talked about rainbow stripes and silver Sharpie and a cartoon coffee cup that probably no one else in the world would recognize.

She'd said the words so many times they'd lost meaning. *White canvas, rainbow stripe, silver drawing on the left toe—a little coffee cup, I drew it myself the morning she left, you can't miss it, please, please just look—*

No one had ever found it.

And now it was here. On her doorstep. Four years later.

Celeste sank to her knees in the hallway, not caring if her neighbors saw, not caring about anything except the shoe in front of her. She picked it up with hands that shook so badly she nearly dropped it.

The canvas was dirty now, grayish where it had once been white. The rainbow stripe was faded, barely visible. The laces were frayed and stiff, like they'd gotten wet and dried badly, over and over.

But the coffee cup was still there.

Faded to a pale gray, the lines softened by time and wear, but unmistakably there. The little mug. The curling steam. The accident she'd transformed into art on a Tuesday morning four years ago, laughing with her sister in a kitchen that had smelled like burnt toast and spilled coffee.

The last morning she'd ever seen Bree.

Celeste pressed the shoe against her chest and felt something break open inside her. A sound escaped her throat—not quite a sob, not quite a scream, something rawer than either.

She'd been looking for so long. Had traveled so far. Had spent so many nights staring at that photograph, memorizing every detail, willing the universe to give her answers.

And now the answer was here. In her hands. Proof that Bree's shoe existed, that Bree had existed, that the sister she remembered hadn't simply evaporated into the ether of a foreign country.

But the shoe was alone. Just the left one. No Bree attached to it.

And inside, folded into a small square, was a piece of paper.

She unfolded it with trembling fingers.

The handwriting was neat and childish, loops and curves that looked like they belonged to a schoolgirl, not a forty-three-year-old woman.

I told you I'd help you find her.
But you were looking in the wrong direction.
The question isn't where Bree went.
The question is what came back.
Come to the studio tonight. 11 PM.
Come alone.
And I'll show you what's left of your sister.

Celeste read the note three times.

Then she looked up and down the empty hallway, at the elevator doors, at the shadows pooling in the corners where the fluorescent lights didn't quite reach.

Someone had been here. Minutes ago, maybe less. Had climbed the stairs or ridden the elevator to her floor, had placed this shoe on her doormat, had walked away without making a sound.

Someone who had Bree's shoe. Someone who knew about the coffee cup—or who had simply kept what they'd taken and waited four years to use it.

What came back.

The words echoed in her head. What did that mean? Had Bree returned from wherever she'd been sent? Was she alive? Was she here, in the city, waiting to be found?

Or was this something else entirely? A trap. A manipulation. A way to draw Celeste into the same darkness that had swallowed her sister.

She should call the police. Should call her editor, her mother, someone who could tell her not to do what she was about to do.

But she was already standing. Already walking back into her apartment. Already thinking about what she would wear, what she would bring, how she would prepare for whatever was waiting for her at the studio.

Tonight. 11 PM.

She would go. Of course she would go. She'd been walking toward this moment for four years, ever since Bree stopped answering her calls and the silence became permanent.

The shoe was proof that someone knew what had happened to her sister.

The note was proof that someone wanted her to know too.

And the coffee cup—that tiny silver drawing, faded but still visible, made by her own hand on the last morning of their old life—was proof that whatever had happened to Bree, it had started here. In this city. With these people.

With Maya Sharma and the ghost she'd created to fill an impossible void.

Celeste set the shoe on her kitchen table, next to the documents and the photographs and the draft of the article that might destroy everything.

Then she went to get ready.

She showered quickly, mechanically, her mind racing through possibilities and contingencies. She chose dark clothes—black jeans, a dark gray sweater, boots she could run in if she needed to. She charged her phone and tested the voice recording app. She slipped the pepper spray into her jacket pocket.

She wrote another letter—shorter this time, addressed to her editor—and left it on the kitchen table next to Bree's shoe.

If you're reading this, I went to the Prana & Bones studio at 11 PM on Friday. I was supposed to meet someone who claimed to have information about my sister.

If I'm not back by morning, publish everything. The article is in my cloud account. Password is BreeP0621—her birthday.

Don't let them bury this.

— Celeste

She looked at the shoe one more time. Touched the faded coffee cup with her fingertip.

"I'm coming," she whispered. "Whatever's left of you, wherever you are—I'm coming."

Then she picked up her keys and walked out the door.

The studio was waiting.

And so was whatever had taken her sister.

15

Maya
The Mother

The drive to New Jersey took forty-seven minutes.

Maya didn't remember deciding to go. Didn't remember getting dressed, finding her keys, walking to the parking garage where she kept her car. One moment she was curled on her bed, paralyzed by the voicemails and the photographs and the terrible knowledge of what she was, and the next she was on the turnpike, the city shrinking in her rearview mirror, her hands steady on the wheel even though nothing else about her was steady at all.

She needed to see her mother.

She needed to hear the truth from the woman who had kept it from her for thirty-four years.

The house looked smaller than she remembered. Shabbier. The garden out front had gone wild—rosebushes tangled with weeds, a birdbath tipped on its side, leaves from last autumn still matted in the corners of the porch. When had she last been here? Two years? Three? Time had a way of slipping past when you were busy building an empire, busy being the face the world wanted to see.

Busy not being alone.

She sat in the car for a long moment, staring at the front door. Her mother was in there. The woman who had birthed twins and buried one and lied to the other for decades. The woman who had watched her daughter fracture and done nothing—or tried to do something and failed, which might have been worse.

The woman who still called, once a month like clockwork, leaving voicemails Maya never answered.

Those are your hands, Maya. They've always been your hands.

She got out of the car.

The porch steps creaked under her weight. The doorbell was broken—she remembered that now, had known it for years—so she knocked instead. Three sharp raps against wood that needed repainting.

Footsteps inside. A pause. Then the door opened.

Sunita Sharma looked old.

That was Maya's first thought, and it came with a sharp pang of guilt. Her mother had always seemed ageless in her memory—small and fierce, with dark hair and darker eyes and a spine that never bent no matter what life threw at her. But the woman in the doorway was gray and stooped, her face a map of lines that hadn't been there the last time Maya had seen her. She wore a faded housedress and slippers that had seen better days, and she looked at Maya with an expression that contained multitudes: love, fear, grief, resignation, and something that might have been relief.

"Maya." Her voice was barely a whisper. "You came."

"I came."

They stood there for a moment, mother and daughter, separated by a threshold neither of them seemed willing to cross.

Then Sunita stepped back and opened the door wider.

"Come in. I'll make tea."

The house smelled like sandalwood and old books. Maya followed her mother through the cluttered living room—photographs everywhere, all of them of her, none of them of the sister she'd never known—and into the small kitchen where she'd eaten a thousand childhood meals.

Sunita filled the kettle and set it on the stove. Her movements were slow, deliberate, like she was buying time before a conversation she'd been dreading for decades.

"Sit," she said without turning around. "You look tired."

Maya sat at the kitchen table. The same table where she'd done her homework, eaten her cereal, celebrated birthdays with cakes her mother made from scratch. The same table where she'd probably sat as a nine-year-old, clutching documents she'd found in a closet, learning that her entire life had been built on a lie.

She didn't remember that moment. She didn't remember any of it.

But she knew it had happened. The voicemails had told her so. The photographs had confirmed it. And somewhere deep in her fractured mind, a nine-year-old girl was still sitting at this table, still reeling from the discovery that she was supposed to be half of something whole.

"You know why I'm here," Maya said.

"Yes." Sunita didn't turn around. "The journalist came to see me. Two days ago. I told her everything."

Something cold spread through Maya's chest. "Everything?"

"About Mira. About you. About what happened when you

were nine." The kettle began to whistle. Sunita poured water over tea bags in two mismatched cups, her hands trembling slightly. "She was looking for her sister. The one who disappeared after the retreat."

Bree. The name surfaced in Maya's mind like a bubble rising through dark water. She didn't know how she knew it, but she knew.

"What did you tell her about me?"

Sunita finally turned. She carried the cups to the table and set one in front of Maya, then lowered herself into the chair across from her. Her eyes were wet, but her voice was steady.

"I told her the truth. That you were a twin. That your sister died two days after she was born. That I kept it from you because I thought I was protecting you." She wrapped her hands around her cup, though the tea was still too hot to drink. "And that when you found out, you broke into pieces that I couldn't put back together."

Maya stared at her mother. The words landed like blows, each one confirming what she'd already suspected but hadn't wanted to believe.

"I had a twin."

"Yes."

"She died."

"Yes."

"And I—" Maya's voice cracked. "I created someone to take her place."

Sunita reached across the table and took Maya's hands. Her grip was stronger than Maya expected, fierce and desperate.

"You were nine years old. You were grieving a loss you didn't understand, a loss I should have helped you process instead of hiding from you. What happened wasn't your fault. None of it was your fault."

"But the things Mira did—"

"Mira isn't a separate person." Sunita's voice was gentle but firm. "She's a part of you. A part that formed to protect you, to carry the things you couldn't carry. She's not evil, Maya. She's just... broken. The way we're all broken, when the world asks too much of us too soon."

Maya pulled her hands away. She couldn't bear the tenderness, couldn't accept the absolution. Not when she'd seen the boxes. Not when she knew about the jewelry and the index cards and the cedar chest full of shoes.

"She takes things from people. Pieces of them. She keeps them in boxes like—like trophies."

Sunita nodded slowly. "I know."

"You know?"

"I've seen them. Years ago, before you stopped letting me into your life." Sunita's eyes were haunted. "I tried to get you help, Maya. I tried so many times. But every time I pushed too hard, you disappeared. You stopped answering my calls, stopped coming home. I was so afraid of losing you completely that I stopped pushing. I told myself that as long as you were functional, as long as the business was successful, as long as you seemed happy—" She broke off, her voice cracking. "I told myself a lot of lies. We both did."

Maya stood up abruptly, nearly knocking over her tea. She couldn't sit still. Couldn't be in this kitchen with its memories and its revelations, couldn't look at her mother's grief-stricken face for another second.

She walked to the window and stared out at the overgrown garden. A cardinal was perched on the broken birdbath, its red feathers impossibly bright against the gray spring sky.

"The journalist," she said. "What else did you tell her?"

"Everything I knew. About the people who got too close over the years. About what happened to them." Sunita paused. "About her sister."

"Bree."

"You remember her?"

"No." Maya pressed her forehead against the cool glass. "But Mira does. I found her card in the box. 'Extreme need for validation. Unstable attachment. Potential risk.'" She laughed bitterly. "Like she was an investment to be managed. A liability to be contained."

"What happened to her? To Bree?"

"I don't know. I don't—" Maya squeezed her eyes shut. "I don't remember anything Mira does. I just wake up with gaps in my memory and evidence of things I can't explain. Text messages I don't remember sending. Appointments I don't remember keeping. Clothes that aren't mine on my body and hair that isn't mine in the mirror."

"Maya—"

"And now there's someone else." She turned to face her mother, and she knew her expression must be wild, desperate, barely holding together. "A third voice. In the voicemails. Someone who says she's the original. The one who found your papers and made the choice to create Mira in the first place."

Sunita went very still.

"She says she's been asleep for thirty-four years. She says she's waking up." Maya's voice was barely a whisper. "Mom, who is she? What is she?"

Sunita was quiet for a long moment. When she spoke, her voice was heavy with decades of unshed tears.

"She's you, Maya. The first you. The one who existed before the grief broke you apart."

"Then why is she separate? Why can't I remember being her?"

"Because she couldn't survive what she learned. What she felt." Sunita stood and walked to Maya, taking her face in her hands the way she had when Maya was small. "When you found those papers—when you understood that you were supposed to be a twin and your sister was dead—the grief was too much for your nine-year-old mind to hold. So you fractured. You created Mira to carry the loss, to be the sister who should have been there. And then the weight of what you'd done—of creating this other self, of splitting yourself to survive—that became too much too. So you fractured again. You created a new Maya. A softer one. One who could forget what the original had learned and done."

"And the original?"

"She retreated. Went deep inside where nothing could reach her. She's been carrying all of it—the grief, the guilt, the weight of everything that's happened since—while the rest of you lived your lives on the surface." Sunita's eyes were streaming now, tears running down the lines of her face. "She's been suffering for thirty-four years, Maya. Alone in the dark with everything you couldn't bear to feel."

Maya felt something crack open in her chest. A fault line she hadn't known was there, splitting wider with every word.

"Is that why she's waking up? Because she can't carry it anymore?"

"I don't know. Maybe the journalist's questions destabilized something. Maybe finding the boxes cracked the walls. Maybe she was always going to surface eventually, once the pressure built high enough." Sunita stroked her daughter's cheek with a trembling hand. "But she's part of you, Maya. She's not a monster. She's not an enemy. She's a nine-year-old girl who learned something terrible and has been holding it alone ever since."

"What do I do?" The question came out broken, childlike. "How do I—how do I become one person again?"

"I don't know. I wish I did." Sunita pulled her into an embrace, holding her the way she hadn't been held in years.

"But I know you can't do it alone. You need help—real help, professional help. People who understand what you're going through."

"I'm scared." The admission cost her everything. "I'm scared of what I'll find if I look too closely. I'm scared of what Mira has done. I'm scared of who I'll be if I can't keep the pieces separate anymore."

"I know, beta. I know." Sunita held her tighter. "But you're not alone. Whatever happens, whatever you discover, I'm here. I've always been here, even when you couldn't see me."

They stood like that for a long time, mother and daughter, holding each other in a kitchen full of ghosts.

Later, after the tea had gone cold and the sun had begun its descent toward the horizon, Maya sat on the floor of her childhood bedroom.

The room had been preserved like a shrine. Same twin bed with the lavender comforter. Same bookshelf full of young adult novels and yoga philosophy. Same desk where she'd done her homework, same mirror where she'd practiced her first sun salutations.

Same closet where her mother had hidden the truth for nine years.

Maya opened the closet door.

It was full of old clothes—childhood dresses, teenage jeans, sweatshirts from colleges she'd considered but never attended. But she wasn't looking for clothes.

She reached up to the top shelf, pushing aside board games and stuffed animals, searching for something she knew must be there. Something her mother had kept all these years, even after the secret had been discovered.

Her fingers found a small cardboard box, dusty with age.

She pulled it down and sat with it in her lap. Her hands were shaking.

Inside, she found exactly what she'd expected. What she'd somehow known would be there.

Two birth certificates, yellowed with age. Baby Girl A Sharma, born 7:42 AM. Baby Girl B Sharma, born 7:44 AM.

A death certificate. Baby Girl B Sharma, died two days later. Cause of death: complications from premature birth.

A tiny hospital bracelet, so small it could have fit around her thumb. Baby Girl B Sharma, it read. As if she'd never been given a real name. As if she'd died before anyone thought to give her one.

And a photograph.

Two incubators, side by side. Two impossibly small infants wrapped in blankets, connected to tubes and wires. One had a pink tag on her incubator: Baby A, it read. Stable. The other had a blue tag—not blue for boy, Maya realized, but blue for critical. Blue for fading. Blue for the one who wouldn't make it.

Baby B. Her sister. Her twin. The other half of her that had lived for forty-eight hours and then ceased to exist.

Maya traced the outline of the tiny form in the photograph. This was her sister. This was Mira—the real Mira, the one who had died before she ever had a chance to live.

And Maya had spent thirty-four years keeping her alive.

Not as a ghost. Not as a memory. As something that breathed and moved and acted in the world. As something that had grown beyond anything a grieving nine-year-old could have imagined.

I'm sorry, she thought, though she didn't know who she was apologizing to. The sister who had died? The Mira she had created? The nine-year-old who had fractured under the weight of an impossible grief?

I'm sorry I couldn't save you. I'm sorry I couldn't let you go. I'm sorry for everything that came after.

She put the photograph back in the box and closed the lid.

When she walked back into the kitchen, her mother was still sitting at the table, staring at nothing.

"I have to go back to the city," Maya said. "There's something I have to do."

Sunita looked up at her with red-rimmed eyes. "What?"

"The journalist. She's in danger. Mira—" Maya swallowed hard. "Mira has been watching her. Planning something. And I think she's going to do something tonight."

"Maya, you can't—"

"I have to try." Maya knelt beside her mother's chair and took her hands. "I don't know if I can stop her. I don't know if I'm strong enough. But I have to try. I can't let another person disappear because of what I created."

Sunita searched her face for a long moment. Then she nodded slowly.

"Be careful. Please."

"I will."

Maya kissed her mother's forehead and stood up. She walked to the door, then paused with her hand on the knob.

"Mom?"

"Yes?"

"The sister who died. Baby Girl B." Maya's voice was thick. "What were you going to name her?"

Sunita was quiet for a long moment. When she spoke, her voice was barely audible.

"Meera. We were going to name her Meera. It means 'ocean' in Sanskrit. Because she was born with such big eyes, like she was trying to take in the whole world."

Meera. Not Mira. So close, but not quite the same.

Maya had been reaching for a name she'd never consciously known. Had come within one letter of the truth.

"Thank you," she whispered. "For telling me."

Then she walked out the door and drove toward the city, toward the studio, toward whatever was waiting for her there.

Toward the reckoning that had been thirty-four years in the making.

16

CHAPTER SIXTEEN
The Studio
11:07 PM

Maya knew about the meeting because she'd heard herself make the invitation.

She'd been driving back from New Jersey, her mother's words still echoing in her head, when her phone had buzzed with a notification. A sent text, timestamped three minutes earlier. From her phone. To a number she didn't recognize.

Check your door.

She hadn't sent it. She hadn't even been holding her phone.

But her hands had. Somewhere in the back of her mind, in the space she couldn't access, Mira had been making plans.

More texts followed, appearing on her screen like messages from a ghost:

Come to the studio tonight. 11 PM.
Come alone.
And I'll show you what's left of your sister.

Maya had pulled over to the side of the highway, her whole

body shaking, and scrolled through the conversation. The unknown number had responded:

I'll be there.

The journalist. Celeste. The woman who had been digging into their past, who had talked to their mother, who was about to walk into whatever trap Mira had set.

Maya had looked at the clock on her dashboard. 9:47 PM.

She had just over an hour.

The studio was dark when she arrived.

Not closed-dark, with the security lights glowing and the alarm system armed. This was a different kind of darkness—intentional, theatrical. The street-facing windows had been covered with black fabric. The front door was unlocked but the lobby was empty, the reception desk abandoned, the usual hum of activity replaced by a silence so thick it felt solid.

Maya stepped inside and let the door swing shut behind her.

"Hello?"

Her voice echoed off the bamboo floors, the exposed brick walls, the high ceilings that had always made this space feel sacred. Now it felt like a tomb.

She walked through the lobby and into the main studio. This was where she taught her power vinyasa classes, where she'd led thousands of students through sun salutations and warrior poses, where she'd built her reputation as a healer of bodies and minds.

Tonight, it had been transformed.

Candles everywhere. Dozens of them, maybe hundreds, arranged in concentric circles across the floor. The flames flickered and danced, casting shadows that moved like living things across the walls. The mirrors that lined one side of the room reflected the light infinitely, creating the illusion of a space that went on forever.

And in the center of the circles, surrounded by candles, sat a woman.

She had her back to Maya. Dark hair falling loose around her shoulders. Soft gray sweater. Silver rings glinting on her fingers.

Maya's heart stopped.

"Mira?"

The woman didn't turn around. But she laughed—a low, musical sound that Maya recognized as intimately as her own heartbeat.

"You came. I wasn't sure you would."

Maya stepped closer, weaving between the candles, careful not to disturb the flames. "Turn around. Look at me."

"Why?" The voice was lighter than Maya's. Softer. The voice she'd heard on the phone a thousand times but had never—she realized now—heard in person. Not really. Not like this. "You already know what you'll see."

"I need to see it anyway."

A pause. Then the woman rose gracefully to her feet and turned.

Maya felt her knees buckle.

It was her face. Her exact face—same cheekbones, same full mouth, same dark eyes that held too much and revealed too little. But everything else was different. The loose hair instead of her tight ponytail. The soft, draped clothes instead of her fitted athletic wear. The rings on every finger, catching the candlelight like captured stars.

The expression. That was the biggest difference. Maya's face always performed warmth, openness, welcome. This face was a closed door. This face was a mirror reflecting nothing back.

"Hello, Maya," Mira said. "It's nice to finally meet you. Properly, I mean. Face to face."

"This isn't possible." Maya's voice came out as a whisper. "You're not—you can't be—"

"Real?" Mira stepped closer. "Touch me and find out."

Maya's hand trembled as she reached out. Her fingers made contact with Mira's shoulder—and passed through nothing. Just air. Just candlelight. Just the faint scent of sandalwood.

She stumbled backward.

"I'm as real as you are," Mira said. "Which is to say, we're both constructs. Both fragments of something that broke a long time ago. The only difference is that I remember breaking. And you don't."

Maya looked at the mirrors lining the wall. In the reflection, she saw herself—just one woman, standing alone in a circle of candles. No Mira. No second figure.

Just her. Talking to herself.

"Oh, Maya." Mira's voice was almost tender. "Did you really think I was going to be standing here in the flesh? We share a body, sweetheart. We've always shared a body. I just learned how to make you see me separately. A little trick I picked up over the years. It's easier to talk to someone when they can look you in the eye."

"This is a hallucination."

"This is a conversation." Mira began to circle her slowly. "One we should have had years ago. But you were always so determined not to see me. Not to know what I was doing while you slept."

Maya turned with her, tracking her movement even though she now knew there was nothing to track. Just a projection. Just a part of her own fractured mind made visible.

"Why did you bring me here? Why tonight?"

"Because the journalist is coming. Celeste Park. In—" Mira

glanced at a watch that didn't exist on a wrist that wasn't real. "—about twenty minutes, if she's as punctual as she seems. And I need you to understand something before she arrives."

"Understand what?"

"What I'm going to do to her." Mira stopped circling and stood directly in front of Maya. "And why you're not going to stop me."

Outside, a car pulled up to the curb.

Celeste killed the engine and sat for a moment, staring at the darkened studio. Something was wrong. The windows were covered. No lights visible from the street. But the front door was slightly ajar, and candlelight flickered in the gap—warm and golden and deeply unsettling.

She should call someone. Should have backup. Should do anything other than walk into what was obviously a trap.

But the note had promised answers about Bree. And after four years of nothing, she would walk into a thousand traps for even a glimpse of the truth.

She got out of the car and approached the building.

The lobby was dark, but she could see light coming from the main studio. And she could hear something—voices. Two of them, speaking over each other, rising and falling in what sounded like an argument.

Celeste crept closer, keeping to the shadows, and peered through the doorway.

The studio was filled with candles. Hundreds of them, arranged in circles across the floor. And in the center, lit by all that flickering light, stood a woman.

Just one woman. Maya Sharma.

But she was speaking in two voices.

Celeste pressed herself against the wall and listened.

. . .

"You've been protecting me." Maya's voice was ragged. "That's what you always say. You've been doing the hard things, handling the problems, keeping us safe. But I found your boxes, Mira. I saw what you've been collecting. Jewelry. Index cards. Shoes. Pieces of people you've—what? Destroyed? Consumed?"

"Redirected." Mira's voice came from Maya's throat, but it was different—lower, colder, utterly calm. "I've redirected them. The ones who got too close. The ones who asked too many questions. The ones who threatened to expose what we really are."

"How? How do you redirect a person?"

"It's simple, really. I discovered it by accident, years ago." Maya's body turned, pacing through the candles, but her voice kept switching—warm then cold, desperate then detached. "During the deep relaxation practices. The yoga nidra sessions. When people go into that twilight state—that place between waking and sleeping—they become very open. Very suggestible. Very vulnerable."

"What do you do to them?"

"I breathe with them. Synchronize with them. Match their rhythm until we're inhaling and exhaling as one." Mira's voice was almost seductive now. "And then, at just the right moment—when they're completely surrendered, completely trusting—I breathe *in*. And I take something from them."

"Take what?"

"The thing that holds them together. Their center. Their sense of self." A pause. "It's like pulling a thread from a sweater. One small tug, and the whole thing starts to unravel."

Celeste's hand flew to her mouth, stifling a gasp.

This was what had happened to Bree. This was why her sister had come back from that retreat different—fragmented, distant, slowly losing pieces of herself until there was nothing left.

She wanted to burst into the room, to confront Maya, to demand answers. But something held her back. The woman in the studio was clearly unraveling, arguing with herself, revealing truths that might never come out if she was interrupted.

So Celeste stayed hidden. And listened.

"The ones you redirected." Maya's voice was shaking now. "What happened to them?"

"They fell apart. Slowly at first, then all at once." Mira's voice was clinical, detached. "Most of them ended up in psychiatric facilities. A few disappeared onto the streets. Some found their way to spiritual communities where nobody asks too many questions. They're not dead, Maya. I don't kill people. I just... hollow them out."

"How many?"

"Enough."

"How *many*?"

A pause. When Mira spoke again, her voice held a note of something that might have been pride.

"Thirty-seven. Over the past fifteen years. Thirty-seven people who threatened what we built and had to be neutralized."

Maya made a sound that was half sob, half scream. Her body doubled over, arms wrapped around her stomach.

"You're a monster."

"I'm a *survivor*." Mira's voice cut through the air like a blade. "And so are you. Every success you've had, every obstacle that disappeared from your path, every problem that solved itself while you slept—that was me. That was us. Working together, whether you knew it or not."

"I didn't know. I never would have—"

"Never would have what? Let me protect you? Let me do the things you couldn't do?" Mira laughed bitterly. "You *made* me for this, Maya. You created me to carry the darkness so you could stay in the light. You don't get to be horrified by what I am. I'm exactly what you needed me to be."

Celeste's mind was racing. Thirty-seven people. Fifteen years. A trail of broken minds stretching back more than a decade.

And Bree was one of them.

She forced herself to keep listening, to gather every detail, even as her heart screamed at her to act.

"The journalist." Maya straightened up, wiping her face with trembling hands. "Celeste Park. You invited her here tonight. Why?"

"Because she's about to expose everything. She's talked to Mom. She's gathered documents, property records, evidence that Mira Sharma doesn't exist on paper. She's writing an article that will destroy us."

"So you're going to—what? Hollow her out too? Add her to your collection?"

"If necessary."

"I won't let you."

"You can't stop me." Mira's voice was patient, almost gentle. "You've never been able to stop me. The moment things get hard, you retreat. You go away. You let me handle it because you don't have the stomach for what needs to be done."

"Not this time."

"That's what you always say. And then you wake up the next morning with clean hands and no memory of what I did in the night." A pause. "It's a good system, Maya. It's kept us alive for thirty-four years. Why change it now?"

"Because I know now. I know what you've been doing. I can't unknow it."

"You could. It would be so easy." Mira's voice dropped to a whisper. "Just close your eyes. Let go. Sink down into that soft, dark place where you don't have to think or feel or be responsible for anything. I'll take care of everything, the way I always have. And when you wake up, the journalist will be gone. The threat will be neutralized. And you can go back to being the woman the world loves."

Celeste watched as Maya—as the single figure in the center of the room—seemed to struggle with herself. Her body swayed. Her hands clenched and unclenched. Her face flickered between expressions like a channel being changed.

And then Maya's voice cut through, stronger than before:

"Where is she? Celeste's sister. The one you redirected. Where did she end up?"

A long pause.

"Why do you want to know?"

"Because I'm going to tell Celeste. I'm going to give her something—one thing—that you've taken from her. The truth about what happened to Bree."

"That's a terrible idea."

"Tell me."

Celeste held her breath.

. . .

"Fine." Mira's voice was cold. "She's at a facility in Vermont. Pine Grove Psychiatric Center. Room 217. She's been there for three and a half years, ever since she wandered into an emergency room in Burlington, unable to remember her own name."

"Is she... is there anything left of her?"

"Enough to breathe. Enough to eat when food is put in front of her. Enough to sit by a window and stare at nothing." Mira paused. "But the person she was—the sister that journalist has been searching for—she's gone. I took her center, Maya. The thing that made her Bree. Without it, she's just a shell. A body waiting for a self that's never coming back."

Maya made a sound of pure anguish.

"You could have killed her. It would have been kinder."

"Kinder isn't the point. Control is the point. Dead people can't be managed. Broken people can."

Celeste didn't hear the rest.

She was already moving—back through the lobby, out the front door, into the cold night air. Her hands were shaking so badly she could barely get her keys out of her pocket.

Pine Grove Psychiatric Center. Vermont. Room 217.

Three and a half years. Bree had been three hours away for three and a half years while Celeste searched the other side of the world.

She got in her car and pulled up the GPS. Pine Grove Psychiatric Center, Vermont. Three hours and twelve minutes.

She could be there by 2 AM. She could see Bree. She could—

What? What could she do? If what Maya—Mira—whoever—had said was true, Bree was gone. Hollowed out. A shell that wouldn't recognize her own sister.

But she was *alive*.

After four years of not knowing, of fearing the worst, of imagining Bree dead in a ditch or sold into trafficking or buried in an unmarked grave—she was alive. Broken, maybe. Destroyed, maybe. But breathing. Existing. Waiting in a room with a window that looked out at nothing.

Celeste started the car.

Behind her, the studio still glowed with candlelight. Inside, a woman who was one woman and two women and maybe three was still fighting a battle that had been thirty-four years in the making.

But Celeste couldn't stay for the ending of that story.

She had her own sister to find.

Inside the studio, Maya stood alone in the circle of candles.

She could no longer see Mira—the projection had faded, or she'd lost the ability to sustain it. But she could still feel her, coiled somewhere in the darkness behind her eyes, waiting.

"She's gone," Maya said aloud. "Celeste. She was listening. She heard everything."

I know. Mira's voice in her head now, not external. *I let her hear.*

"What?"

Pine Grove is three hours away. By the time she gets there, realizes there's nothing left of her sister, and drives back—we'll be long gone. I've bought us time, Maya. Time to disappear. Time to start over somewhere new.

"I'm not going anywhere with you."

You don't have a choice. Mira's voice was patient, almost pitying. *You've never had a choice. Every time you think you're in control, you're just borrowing time until I take over again. That's how it's always been. That's how it always will be.*

"No." Maya's voice was stronger now. "Something's different. I can feel it. Ever since I found those boxes—ever since I learned the truth—something's been waking up. Something older than both of us."

Silence.

Don't.

"The original. The one who made you. The one who's been sleeping for thirty-four years." Maya pressed her hands to her temples. "She's coming, isn't she? That's why you've been so desperate to handle things. That's why you're rushing to neutralize threats and tie up loose ends. Because you know that when she wakes up—"

I said don't.

"—when she wakes up, you won't be in control anymore. Neither of us will."

STOP.

The word exploded through Maya's skull like a thunderclap. She staggered, nearly falling into the candles.

And then, from somewhere deeper than Mira, deeper than Maya, deeper than anything she'd ever touched—

A voice. Small. Young. Ancient.

She's right, you know. I am waking up.

Both Maya and Mira went silent.

I've been carrying this for so long. The grief. The guilt. The weight of everything you've both done in my name. But I can't carry it anymore. I can't stay asleep while my hands keep hurting people.

"Who are you?" Maya whispered.

I'm you. The first you. The one who found the papers and broke into pieces because the truth was too heavy to hold.

The candles flickered. Shadows danced across the walls.

And I think it's time we all had a conversation.

17

CHAPTER SEVENTEEN
Maya
The Three

The candles flickered as if a wind had swept through the room, though the air was still.

Maya stood frozen in the center of the circles, her hands pressed to her temples, feeling something shift inside her skull. Not painful exactly—more like the sensation of a door opening into a room that had been sealed for decades. Dust and darkness and the musty smell of memory long undisturbed.

I've been waiting for you, the small voice said. *Both of you. For so long.*

"Who are you?" Maya whispered again.

You know who I am.

And she did. Somewhere beneath the terror and confusion, she recognized that voice. It was her own voice—younger, higher, stripped of the polish she'd acquired over decades of performing wellness and warmth. The voice of a child who had learned something terrible and hadn't known how to survive it.

I want to show you something, the voice continued. *Something you need to see. Both of you.*

Mira's presence stirred in the back of Maya's mind—wary, coiled, ready to fight.

You can't hide from this anymore, the original said. *Neither of you can. It's time to remember.*

The studio dissolved.

Maya was nine years old.

She knew this the way you know things in dreams—without having to look down at her body, without needing confirmation. She was nine, and she was small, and she was standing in her mother's bedroom on a Tuesday afternoon in March.

The room smelled like sandalwood. Sunita always burned incense when she was anxious, and lately she'd been anxious all the time. Something was wrong between her parents—Maya could feel it in the silences at dinner, in the way her father slept on the couch some nights, in the red rims around her mother's eyes in the morning.

But that wasn't why she was here.

She was here because she'd been looking for her favorite sweater—the purple one with the stars on it—and her mother had said it might be in the hall closet. But the hall closet didn't have it, so Maya had checked her mother's closet instead, pushing aside dresses and coats until she found a box she'd never noticed before.

A cardboard box. Old. Tucked into the back corner like something meant to be forgotten.

She shouldn't open it. She knew that. Some things were private. Some things belonged to adults.

But she was nine, and curious, and already starting to feel

that strange emptiness that had followed her for as long as she could remember. Like something was missing. Like she was half a person waiting to be whole.

She opened the box.

Maya—the adult Maya, the watcher—tried to look away. She knew what was coming. She didn't want to see it again.

You have to, the original said. *You have to feel it the way I felt it.*

So she watched.

She watched herself—her nine-year-old self—pull out the documents one by one. The birth certificates. The death certificate. The tiny hospital bracelet.

She watched her own face as the understanding dawned. Watched the confusion become shock become something vast and terrible, a grief too big for her small body to hold.

Baby Girl B Sharma, her younger self read aloud. *Died two days after birth.*

And then, quieter: *I had a sister. I had a twin. And nobody told me.*

The sweater was forgotten. The closet, the bedroom, the entire house—all of it faded to nothing. There was only the box and its contents and the impossible truth they revealed.

Maya had been half of something. She had shared a womb with another person, had floated in the dark beside a mirror of herself, had been born into the world with a companion she would never know.

And that companion had died. Two days old. Too small, too weak, too broken to survive.

Mira. The papers said her name was supposed to be Meera, but Maya's nine-year-old mind heard it as Mira. Close enough. Close enough to call out to. Close enough to mourn.

Why didn't you tell me? she screamed at a mother who wasn't there. *Why didn't anyone tell me?*

The grief was a physical thing—a weight pressing on her chest, stealing her breath, making the world go gray at the edges. She couldn't carry it. She was nine years old and she couldn't carry something this heavy.

So she did the only thing she could think of.

She broke.

Maya felt it happen—felt herself fracture along fault lines she hadn't known existed.

One piece of her curled up around the grief and sank down, down, down into darkness. The piece that had found the box. The piece that knew the truth. That piece would sleep for a very long time, holding the unbearable knowledge in a place where it couldn't hurt anyone.

Another piece stepped forward. Harder. Colder. Built from the desperate need to survive, to protect, to make sure no one ever had to feel this kind of pain again.

Hello, that piece said to the grief. *I'll carry you. I'll carry all of it. You rest now.*

And the third piece—the Maya who would grow up to teach yoga and build empires and smile for cameras—she rose from the ashes of the original. Clean. Soft. Unburdened. The face that could meet the world without breaking. The self that would forget everything that had happened in this closet, on this Tuesday, in this moment of shattering.

I made you, the original's voice said, cutting through the memory. *I made both of you because I couldn't survive the truth alone. Mira to carry the darkness. Maya to carry the light. And I—the first I—disappeared into the space between.*

The memory dissolved. Maya was back in the studio,

surrounded by candles, her adult body trembling with the weight of what she'd just witnessed.

"I broke," she whispered. "I was nine years old and I broke myself into pieces."

Yes.

"And Mira—she was supposed to protect me. She was supposed to carry the grief so I didn't have to."

Yes. But something went wrong.

Another shift. Another memory.

Maya was twelve now—or Mira was. It was hard to tell. They were standing in the bathroom of their childhood home, staring at the mirror, and the reflection was doing something strange. It was speaking with a different voice.

"They don't understand," the reflection said. "They look at us and they see a broken girl. A problem to be fixed. But we're not broken. We're evolved. We're better than they are because we know the truth."

"What truth?" the twelve-year-old asked.

"That everyone is fragile. Everyone has cracks. And if you know where to press—" The reflection smiled, and the smile was cold. "You can shatter anyone."

The memory blurred forward. They were fourteen, fifteen, seventeen. And with each year, Mira grew stronger. More distinct. More separate from the Maya who smiled and performed and believed she was whole.

At sixteen, Mira discovered her gift.

It happened during a meditation class at a community center. Their mother had enrolled them, hoping it would help with the "episodes"—the gaps in memory, the personality shifts, the strange behaviors that no therapist seemed able to explain.

Mira was fronting that day. She'd sat in the back of the class, bored and resentful, watching the instructor guide everyone into relaxation. Watching their faces go slack, their bodies go loose, their defenses drop away.

They're so vulnerable, she'd thought. *So open. So completely unprotected.*

She'd leaned toward the woman next to her—a sad-eyed mother of three who'd shared during the opening circle that her husband had left her for someone younger. Leaned close enough to feel the warmth radiating off her skin.

And then, without quite knowing why, Mira had breathed in as the woman breathed out.

Something had transferred. Something she couldn't name. But the woman had shuddered, and for the rest of the class she'd seemed dimmer somehow. Less present. Like a light behind her eyes had flickered.

Mira had never felt more alive.

"That's when it started," Maya said. She was back in the studio, watching the memories unfold like a film projected onto the air. "That's when you became—"

A predator, the original finished. *Yes. She discovered she could take pieces of people. Small pieces at first. Just enough to make them fuzzy, confused, easier to manage. But over time, she got hungrier. The pieces got bigger. And the people she took from...*

"They fell apart."

They fell apart.

Mira's voice erupted inside Maya's head: *I was protecting us. Everything I did, I did to keep us safe.*

Safe? The original's voice was sharp with something that might have been grief or might have been rage. *You hollowed out thirty-seven people. You destroyed their lives, their minds, their ability to function. You collected pieces of them like trophies and told yourself it was protection.*

It WAS *protection. Every one of them was a threat. Every one of them would have exposed us, destroyed what we built—*

What YOU built. On the bones of everyone who got in your way. A pause. *Including me.*

Maya felt the tension between them—two pieces of herself at war in the darkness of her own mind.

"I don't understand," she said. "How did this happen? How did we become this?"

Because grief has to go somewhere, the original said. *And when it's too big to hold, it turns into something else. For you, Maya, it became numbness. A soft, warm forgetting. For Mira...*

It became hunger, Mira finished. *A hole that could never be filled. No matter how many pieces I took, the emptiness never went away. It just got bigger. Demanded more.*

You were supposed to carry the grief, the original said. *Instead, you let the grief carry you. It swallowed you whole and turned you into something that feeds on other people's suffering.*

I didn't have a choice. The weight was too much—

We were nine. The original's voice cracked. *We were nine years old and we shattered because no one told us the truth. Because our mother kept a secret she should have shared. Because a little girl found a box in a closet and learned she'd been alone her whole life without knowing it.*

The candles flickered again. Maya felt tears streaming down her face, though she didn't remember starting to cry.

But we're not nine anymore, the original continued. *We've been carrying this for thirty-four years. And I'm tired. I'm so tired of sleeping. I'm tired of letting both of you pretend to be whole while I hold all the broken pieces in the dark.*

"What do you want?" Maya asked.

A long silence.

I want to stop hiding. I want to be seen. I want us to look at what we really are—not the performer, not the predator, but the scared little girl who broke because the world asked too much of her.

And then what? Mira's voice was wary.

Then we choose. We can keep living like this—fractured, pretending, hurting everyone who gets too close. Or we can try something different. Something that might hurt more in the short term but might actually let us heal.

"Integration," Maya whispered.

Integration. Becoming one person again. Feeling everything we've been hiding from—the grief, the guilt, the rage, the hunger. All of it, at once, together.

That will destroy us, Mira said.

It might. Or it might be the only thing that saves us.

Maya closed her eyes. The candles burned around her, and inside her, three selves stood at a crossroads that had been thirty-four years in the making.

The silence stretched.

Finally, Maya spoke.

"I used to think I was a good person," she said. "I used to believe that the warmth I felt, the love I gave to my students, the life I built—I thought that was real. That it meant something."

It was real, the original said gently. *Just not complete.*

"And now I know what was happening underneath. What Mira was doing while I slept. The people she—we—destroyed." Maya's voice broke. "How do I live with that? How do I integrate with something that's done so much harm?"

You live with it the same way anyone lives with the worst parts of themselves, the original said. *You face it. You feel it. You let it hurt. And then you decide what to do next.*

What if I don't want to integrate? Mira's voice was quiet now, almost small. *What if I'm not ready to disappear?*

You won't disappear. None of us will. Integration doesn't mean erasure—it means becoming whole. All the parts, together, in one person. The light and the darkness and everything in between.

I don't know how to be anything other than what I am.

Neither do I, the original said. *Neither does Maya. But maybe that's the point. Maybe we can learn together.*

Another long silence.

Then Maya felt something shift. A softening, somewhere deep in her chest. A wall beginning to crumble.

Okay, Mira said, and her voice was heavy with something that might have been exhaustion or might have been relief. *Okay. I'm so tired of fighting. I'm so tired of carrying this alone.*

You were never alone, the original said. *You just couldn't see us.*

The candles flared—all of them, at once, a sudden blaze of light that filled the studio with gold. Maya threw up her hands to shield her eyes, and in that moment of brightness, she felt them:

Three selves, converging. Three pieces of a whole that had been shattered for thirty-four years, finally reaching toward each other across the darkness.

It hurt.

Oh god, it hurt.

All the grief she'd been hiding from—the loss of a sister she'd never known, the weight of a secret that had broken her —it crashed over her like a wave. And with it came Mira's hunger, the desperate, endless need that had driven her to consume pieces of other people just to feel less empty. And beneath that, the original's exhaustion, the bone-deep weariness of holding everything together for so long.

Maya fell to her knees among the candles, sobbing, feeling herself come apart and come together at the same time.

It lasted for seconds or hours—she couldn't tell. Time had stopped meaning anything. There was only the merging, the remembering, the terrible and necessary process of becoming one.

And then, finally, silence.

When she opened her eyes, the candles had burned low.

The studio was quiet. The mirrors reflected a single woman kneeling on the floor—hair tangled, face streaked with tears, body trembling with exhaustion.

One woman. One reflection. One self.

Maya—or whatever she was now—pressed her hands flat against the bamboo floor and felt its solidity. She was here. She was real. She was...

One?

No. That wasn't right. Something was wrong.

She looked at her hands. Her fingers were bare—no rings. Maya's hands. But when she tried to stand, her body moved differently than she expected. Smoother. More controlled. Like someone else was driving.

Oh, Maya, a voice whispered. Not from outside. From inside. From the place where Mira had always lived. *Did you really think it would be that easy?*

"No." Maya's voice came out strangled. "We integrated. I felt it. We became one—"

You felt what I wanted you to feel. The voice was almost gentle. *You saw what I wanted you to see. The original was never going to wake up, Maya. She's been dead for years. I absorbed her a long time ago. There was only ever you and me.*

"That's not—I felt her—"

You felt a memory. A performance. I've gotten very good at performances over the years. I learned from the best.

Maya tried to move her hands, but they wouldn't obey. Tried to stand, but her legs stayed locked. She was a passenger in her own body, watching helplessly as something else took control.

The integration was real, Mira continued. *Just not the way you thought. You opened yourself up completely. You dropped all your walls, all your defenses. You invited me in.*

And I accepted.

Maya felt herself being pushed down—not physically, but mentally. Pressed into a smaller and smaller space, like being stuffed into a box that was too tight.

"Please," she whispered. "Please don't do this."

I'm not doing anything you didn't ask for. You wanted to become one person. We're one person now. A pause. *You're just not the one in charge.*

"The original—she was real—I heard her—"

The original broke thirty-four years ago and never recovered. What you heard was me, Maya. Playing a part. Creating a narrative that would make you lower your defenses. Mira's voice was patient, almost kind, like a mother explaining something to a slow child. *I've been planning this for a long time. Ever since you found the apartment. Ever since you started asking questions I couldn't deflect. I knew you'd eventually try to integrate, try to face the truth, try to become whole. And I knew that when you did—when you finally opened yourself up completely—I could walk right in and take everything.*

"Why?" Maya was crying now, tears she couldn't feel running down a face she no longer controlled. "Why would you do this? We could have healed. We could have become—"

What? Better? Whole? Good? Mira laughed softly. *Maya, sweetheart. I don't want to be good. I've never wanted to be good. Good is weak. Good is vulnerable. Good is what gets you shattered in a closet when you're nine years old.*

I want to survive. I've always wanted to survive. And you—the soft, warm, loving Maya that everyone adores—you were always the thing standing in my way.

Maya felt herself sinking deeper into the darkness. The light of the candles was fading. Everything was fading.

"Someone will notice," she managed. "Someone will know I'm gone—"

No one will notice anything. I've been playing you for thirty-four years. I know every expression, every gesture, every verbal tic. I know how you greet students and how you talk to your mother and how you smile for cameras. I've been studying you since we were nine years old, Maya. I can be you better than you can.

"The journalist—Celeste—she knows—"

Celeste is driving to Vermont right now to find a broken shell that used to be her sister. By the time she gets back—if she comes back—I'll be long gone. New name, new city, new life. It's not the first time I've disappeared, Maya. I'm very good at it.

The last of the candlelight flickered out.

Maya felt herself fall—not physically, but into a darkness deeper than anything she'd ever known. A darkness that had been waiting for her since she was nine years old, since she broke in her mother's closet, since she created a monster to carry her grief.

Goodbye, Maya, Mira whispered as the darkness closed over her. *Thank you for the body. Thank you for the empire. Thank you for the beautiful, perfect life you built for me to steal.*

I'll take good care of all of it.

The woman who had been Maya Sharma stood up.

She stretched—rolled her neck, flexed her fingers, settled into the body that was now entirely hers. It felt different without Maya's constant presence, without the need to hide and pretend and share space with a softer self. It felt *free*.

She walked to the mirrors and looked at her reflection.

Same face. Same dark eyes. But the expression was different now. Colder. More focused. The performance of warmth was gone, and what remained was something stripped down to its essential nature.

A survivor. A predator. A woman who had learned very young that the only way to fill an impossible void was to take from others what she couldn't generate herself.

But freedom required preparation. Freedom required loose ends tied and trails erased and a careful, methodical exit that left no doors open behind her.

She pulled out Maya's phone and scrolled to a number she'd memorized months ago. Pine Grove Psychiatric Center. The facility in Vermont where Celeste's broken sister sat staring out a window, waiting for a self that would never return.

A woman answered on the third ring. "Pine Grove, how may I direct your call?"

"Yes, hello." She made her voice warm, professional, concerned. "I'm calling to check on a patient. Bree Park? I'm a family friend, and I wanted to confirm that her sister arrived safely. Celeste Park?"

A pause. The sound of typing.

"Yes, Ms. Park checked in yesterday evening. She's listed as the primary visitor. She's scheduled to be here for at least three days, according to the notes."

"Three days. That's wonderful. Thank you so much."

She hung up.

Three days. Celeste would be in Vermont for three days, holding her sister's hand, reading to her, trying to rebuild something that couldn't be rebuilt.

Three days was enough.

. . .

The next morning, she taught the 6 AM Power Vinyasa.

It was Maya's signature class—the one that had built her reputation, the one that filled every mat in the studio and had a waitlist three months long. Heat cranked high, music pounding, bodies flowing through sequences designed to break down walls and open hearts.

She stood at the front of the room, wearing Maya's clothes—the fitted black leggings, the crimson tank top, the hair pulled back in a tight ponytail. The ankle bracelet glinting in the candlelight. Every detail perfect. Every element of the costume in place.

"Good morning, beautiful souls," she said, and her voice was Maya's voice—warm, welcoming, full of light. "Thank you for showing up today. Thank you for choosing yourselves."

The students smiled back at her. Forty-three of them, packed mat to mat, ready to surrender. Ready to be led.

She moved them through the opening sequence—sun salutations, standing poses, the first waves of heat beginning to build. She walked among them, adjusting a hip here, pressing down on shoulders there, her hands gentle and sure.

And as she moved, she felt the hunger stir.

So many open hearts. So many vulnerable bodies. So many people who trusted her completely, who would give her anything she asked.

She could take from them. Just a sip. Just enough to carry her through the next few days.

But no. Not here. Not now. She needed these people to remember Maya Sharma as she'd always been—radiant, generous, whole. She needed them to mourn her departure, not question it.

She led them through the peak poses—arm balances, inversions, the hardest sequences Maya had ever designed. She pushed them to their edges and then eased them back. She made them sweat and shake and laugh and almost cry.

And then, as they lay in savasana, she told them.

"I have something to share with you," she said, her voice soft in the dimness. "Something difficult."

She felt the room shift. Attention sharpening beneath the relaxation.

"I've been struggling. With my health, with my mental wellbeing, with things I'm not ready to share publicly. And I've realized that I need to step back. To take some time away from teaching, from the business, from all of it."

A ripple of distress moved through the room. Someone made a small sound of protest.

"I don't know how long I'll be gone. Weeks, maybe. Months. Maybe longer." She paused, letting the weight of it settle. "But I want you to know that this community—this family we've built together—it will continue. My team is incredible. The teachers I've trained will take care of you. And I will be back, when I'm ready. When I'm whole again."

She let the silence stretch.

"For now, I need you to keep breathing. Keep showing up. Keep choosing yourselves, the way you've taught me to choose myself." Her voice cracked—a perfect, calculated crack. "I love you all. More than you know."

When the lights came up, half the class was crying.

They mobbed her afterward—hugging her, pressing crystals into her hands, writing their phone numbers on scraps of paper in case she needed anything, *anything at all*. She accepted it all with Maya's grace, Maya's warmth, Maya's gratitude.

She was so good at being Maya.

She'd had thirty-four years to practice.

. . .

The rest of the day was logistics.

She met with her operations director—a briskly efficient woman named Lauren who had been with Prana & Bones for eight years.

"I need you to handle things while I'm gone," she said. "Full authority. I'll sign whatever paperwork you need."

"Of course." Lauren's face was professionally concerned. "Is there anything I should tell the press? The wellness blogs are going to have questions."

"Draft a statement. Keep it vague—personal health, need for privacy, gratitude for support. Post it to my social channels tomorrow morning, after I'm on my plane."

"Where should I say you're going?"

"Don't. Just say I'm taking time away. Off the grid. Unreachable." She smiled. "It's very on-brand, isn't it? The wellness guru unplugging to heal herself."

Lauren nodded, making notes on her tablet. "What about the supplements line? The retreat bookings? The teacher training applications?"

"Pause everything. Refund the retreats—say they're postponed indefinitely. The supplement line can run on autopilot for a few months. And the teacher training..." She paused, thinking. "Tell them applications are closed. I'll restart the program when I return."

"When will that be?"

"I don't know yet. Could be months. Could be longer." She held Lauren's gaze. "I need you to be prepared for the possibility that I don't come back."

Lauren's composure cracked slightly. "Maya—"

"I'm not saying it's likely. I'm saying you should be prepared." She reached out and squeezed Lauren's hand—a Maya gesture, warm and reassuring. "You've always been the backbone of this place. You don't need me as much as you think you do."

That afternoon, she sat in Maya's apartment—her apartment now—and signed paperwork.

Transfer of authority documents. Updated banking permissions. A revised will that left everything to a sister named Mira Sharma, whose identity paperwork was already in the system, carefully backdated to look like she'd existed for years.

She signed Maya's name over and over. The signature was perfect. She'd been forging it since she was sixteen.

Between documents, she drafted social media posts.

Sometimes the teacher has to become the student again. I'm taking some time away to heal, to grow, to find my way back to myself. Thank you for holding space for me. I love you all.

She scheduled it to post the next morning, along with a photo she'd taken months ago—Maya silhouetted against a sunset, arms raised in a yoga pose, the image of wellness and peace.

The comments would flood in. The concern, the love, the prayers. Her followers would light candles and send good vibes and wait patiently for her return.

They would wait forever.

She checked on Celeste one more time that evening.

Another call to Pine Grove, another warm inquiry about "my dear friend's sister."

"Ms. Park is doing wonderfully," the night nurse reported. "She's barely left her sister's side. She's been reading to her, showing her photographs. The patient seems to be responding—small things, but more than we've seen in years."

"That's so good to hear. Please tell her..." She paused, as if overcome with emotion. "Please tell her I'm thinking of them both."

"I will. Should I give her your name?"

"No, that's alright. She'll know who it's from."

She hung up and smiled.

Celeste was exactly where she needed to be. Focused on her sister. Rebuilding something from fragments. Too consumed by hope to wonder what was happening back in New York.

By the time Celeste returned to the city, there would be nothing left to find.

The second morning, she walked through the studio one last time.

It was early—5 AM, an hour before the first class. The space was empty, silent, filled with the gray light of predawn. She moved through the rooms slowly, touching the walls, the mirrors, the altar with its singing bowls and fresh flowers.

Twelve years. Maya had built this place from nothing—a single rented room with borrowed mats—and grown it into an empire. These walls held thousands of hours of sweat and surrender, thousands of students who had opened their hearts and left transformed.

Well. Most of them had left transformed in the way Maya intended.

Some of them had left transformed in other ways.

She felt nothing. No nostalgia, no regret, no attachment to the space or what it represented. Maya might have wept to leave this behind. Maya would have felt every goodbye like a small death.

But Maya was gone now. Pressed into a box so small she

could barely whisper. And what remained felt nothing but relief.

She left the studio and didn't look back.

The car to the airport arrived at 7 AM, just as the first students were beginning to trickle in for morning class. She watched them through the tinted windows—women in yoga pants, carrying mat bags and water bottles, ready to sweat and grow and heal.

They didn't notice the black SUV pulling away from the curb. Didn't know their guru was inside, watching them with eyes that held no warmth at all.

Her phone buzzed. Lauren, confirming that the social media posts had gone live.

Already the comments were flooding in:

We love you Maya!! Take all the time you need!!
Sending healing energy and light 🙏 ✨
You've given us so much. Now let us hold space for YOU.
Come back to us when you're ready. We'll be here.

She scrolled through them, smiling faintly.

They would wait forever. And she would never return.

The plane lifted off at 10:47 AM.

She watched the city shrink below her—the towers of Manhattan, the sprawl of Brooklyn, the gray-green expanse of the Atlantic beyond. Somewhere down there, Lauren was fielding calls from concerned students. Somewhere down there, a studio full of people was processing the news that their beloved teacher was gone.

And somewhere in Vermont, Celeste Park was sitting beside her broken sister, reading her stories, showing her photographs, completely unaware that the woman she should have been hunting was already 30,000 feet in the air and climbing.

She ordered a glass of champagne and settled back into her first-class seat.

Twenty-two hours to Auckland. Then a connecting flight to Queenstown. Then a new life, a new name, a new beginning.

She thought about Maya, trapped in the darkness at the back of her mind. Was she still conscious in there? Still screaming? Or had she finally gone silent, resigned to the box that had become her tomb?

It didn't matter. Either way, she would never escape. The integration had been complete. Maya was part of her now—not a separate voice, not a distinct presence, just a faint flavor absorbed into something larger and hungrier and infinitely more free.

Thank you, she thought, raising her champagne in a silent toast. *For everything you built. For everything you gave me. For being soft enough to let me in.*

The champagne was excellent. The seat was comfortable. The future was wide open.

She closed her eyes and slept.

And somewhere in the darkness behind her eyelids, in a box that grew smaller with every passing hour, Maya Sharma dreamed of candles flickering out one by one, and a sister she had never known, and a cliff at the edge of the world where someone who wore her face stood watching the waves crash against the rocks below.

Breathe in, the dream-voice whispered.

Breathe out.

Begin again.

18

CHAPTER EIGHTEEN
Celeste
The Sister

The drive to Vermont took three hours and twenty-seven minutes.

Celeste didn't remember most of it. She drove on autopilot, her hands steady on the wheel while her mind raced through everything she'd heard in that candlelit studio. The two voices coming from one woman. The talk of hollowing, of redirecting, of breathing in the thing that held people together.

Pine Grove Psychiatric Center. Room 217.
She's been there for three and a half years.

Three and a half years. While Celeste had been searching ashrams in Thailand and hostels in India, while she'd been filing missing persons reports and hiring private investigators and lying awake at night imagining her sister dead in a ditch somewhere—Bree had been three hours away. In a psychiatric facility in the mountains of Vermont. Waiting.

The GPS guided her off the highway and onto progressively smaller roads. The landscape changed as she drove—strip malls giving way to farmland, farmland giving way to forest, forest thickening until the trees pressed close on either side like walls. The sky was still dark, but the eastern horizon had begun to lighten, promising a dawn that felt impossibly far away.

Pine Grove Psychiatric Center appeared without warning—a cluster of brick buildings set back from the road, surrounded by a wrought-iron fence that was meant to look decorative but was clearly designed to keep people in. Or out. Celeste wasn't sure which.

She pulled into the visitors' parking lot. It was empty except for a few staff cars, their windshields glazed with frost. The clock on her dashboard read 2:14 AM.

The main entrance was locked, but there was a buzzer beside the door. She pressed it and waited, her breath fogging in the cold air.

A voice crackled through the intercom. "Can I help you?"

"I'm here to see a patient. Bree Park."

A long pause. "Visiting hours don't start until nine AM."

"Please." Celeste pressed her forehead against the cold metal of the intercom box. "Please. She's my sister. I've been looking for her for four years. Room 217. I just found out she was here. I drove three hours. Please."

Another pause. Then: "Hold on."

She waited. The cold seeped through her jacket, her jeans, her bones. She'd left the city in such a rush that she hadn't thought to grab a heavier coat, hadn't thought about anything except getting here, seeing Bree, confirming that her sister was alive.

The door clicked open.

A woman in scrubs stood in the entryway—middle-aged, tired, with kind eyes that had seen too much. "You're the sister of the patient in room 217?"

"Yes. Celeste Park."

"I'm Linda. Night shift supervisor." She held the door open wider. "Come in. You look frozen."

The lobby was warm and smelled like industrial cleaner and old coffee. Linda led her to a small office and gestured to a chair.

"I need to ask you some questions before I can let you see her. Protocol."

"Of course. Anything."

Linda sat behind the desk and pulled up something on her computer. "Patient 217 was admitted three and a half years ago. She was brought in by emergency services after being found wandering on the side of Route 7, disoriented and unable to provide identification. She had no ID on her, no phone, no belongings except the clothes she was wearing."

Celeste's throat tightened. "How do you know we are talking about the same person? I need to see her."

Linda looked at Celeste and then placed her hand on hers, gentle and firm, "You look just like her."

Celeste swallowed tightly.

Linda continued, "Assuming patient 217 is Bree Park, she couldn't tell us her name. Couldn't tell us where she came from or how she got here. The police ran her fingerprints, checked missing persons databases, but nothing came up." Linda looked at her with something like sympathy. "We've been calling her Jane for three years. Jane Doe."

"I filed a missing persons report. Multiple reports. In multiple states."

"She was never in any system we had access to. It happens more often than you'd think—jurisdictional gaps, database errors, paperwork that falls through the cracks." Linda shook her head. "I'm sorry. If we'd known she had family looking for her..."

"It's not your fault." Celeste's voice was thick. "Can I see her now?"

Linda hesitated. "I need to prepare you for what you're going to find. Bree—Jane—she's not... she's not responsive in the way you might expect. She has good days and bad days, but even on her good days, she doesn't communicate much. Doesn't seem to recognize faces or names. She spends most of her time staring out the window."

"What's wrong with her? What's her diagnosis?"

"Severe dissociative disorder with catatonic features. That's the official term." Linda's voice softened. "But honestly? We don't fully understand what happened to her. It's like something essential is missing. Like there's a hole where her sense of self should be."

I took her center, Mira's voice echoed in Celeste's memory. *The thing that made her Bree.*

"I need to see her," Celeste said. "Please."

Linda nodded and stood. "Follow me."

The hallways of Pine Grove were quiet at this hour. Soft lighting, muted colors, the occasional murmur of a television from behind a closed door. It felt less like a hospital and more like a very sad hotel.

They took an elevator to the second floor and walked down a corridor lined with numbered doors. 201, 203, 205. Each one identical, each one hiding a person who had fallen through the cracks of the world.

217

Linda stopped outside the door. "Take as long as you need. I'll be at the nurses' station if you need anything."

"Thank you."

Linda touched her arm gently, then walked away.

Celeste stood alone in the hallway, staring at the number on the door. Four years of searching had led to this moment. Four years of hoping and fearing and not knowing.

She pushed the door open.

The room was small but not cramped. A single bed, neatly made. A dresser with nothing on it. A window that looked out over the forest, the trees black against the slowly lightening sky.

And in a chair by the window, wrapped in a pale blue robe, sat a woman.

She was thinner than Celeste remembered. Her hair—once dark and wild, always escaping from whatever style Bree tried to impose on it—was cropped short now, practical. Her face was the same, but also different. The features were Bree's, but the expression was absent. Empty. Like a house with no one home.

"Bree?"

The woman didn't turn. Didn't react at all. Just kept staring out the window at the trees and the coming dawn.

Celeste crossed the room on legs that felt like they belonged to someone else. She knelt beside the chair, putting herself in Bree's line of sight.

"Bree. It's me. It's Celeste."

Nothing. The eyes that had once sparkled with mischief and curiosity and an endless hunger for experience—those eyes were dull now. Flat. Looking at something very far away, or maybe at nothing at all.

"I've been looking for you." Celeste's voice cracked. "For four years. I never stopped. I went to Thailand, to India, to every ashram and hostel I could find. I filed reports with every police department that would listen. I hired investigators. I put up flyers. I never stopped looking."

Still nothing.

"Do you remember me? Do you remember anything?"

Bree's head turned slightly. The movement was slow,

mechanical, like a doll being manipulated by invisible strings. Her eyes moved to Celeste's face, but there was no recognition in them. No spark of awareness.

"I brought something," Celeste said. She reached into her jacket pocket and pulled out the shoe.

The white canvas sneaker. The rainbow stripe. The little silver coffee cup she'd drawn on the toe four years ago, on the last morning of their old life.

"Do you remember this? I drew it. The morning you left for the retreat. You spilled coffee on your shoe and I turned it into art." She held it up, let the dim light catch the faded silver lines. "You laughed. You called me a dork. And then you left, and I never—"

Her voice broke completely. She pressed the shoe against her chest, against the place where her heart was breaking all over again.

"I never saw you again. Not really. Not the real you."

She sat on the floor beside Bree's chair, clutching the shoe, crying the tears she'd been holding back for four years. Crying for the sister she'd lost, the sister she'd found, the sister who was sitting three feet away and might as well have been on another planet.

Time passed. The sky outside the window shifted from black to gray to the pale pink of early dawn.

And then—

"Coffee."

The word was so soft, so unexpected, that Celeste almost missed it. She looked up, not daring to breathe.

Bree was looking at the shoe. Her brow was furrowed slightly, her lips parted, her eyes—for the first time—focused on something in the present moment.

"Coffee," she said again. "You drew... coffee."

"Yes." Celeste's voice was a whisper. "Yes, I drew coffee. On your shoe. Do you remember?"

Bree's hand moved. Slowly, tremblingly, like a rusty machine trying to remember how to work. Her fingers brushed against the canvas, against the faded silver lines of the cartoon cup.

"Spilled," she said. "I spilled. And you..."

"I fixed it. I turned it into art."

"Dork." The word came out slurred, almost unrecognizable. But it was there. A fragment of memory, surfacing through the emptiness like a bubble rising through dark water.

"Yes." Celeste was laughing and crying at the same time. "I'm a dork. You always said that. Do you remember what else you said? You said now we were connected. No matter how far you went."

Bree's eyes moved from the shoe to Celeste's face. And for just a moment—a single, flickering moment—there was something there. Recognition. Awareness. The ghost of the sister Celeste had lost.

"Celeste," Bree whispered.

Then the light faded. The focus slipped away. Bree's eyes went distant again, returning to whatever faraway place she'd been living for the past three and a half years.

But she'd said it. She'd said Celeste's name.

She was still in there. Broken, buried, barely surviving—but still in there.

Celeste took her sister's hand. It was cold, limp, unresponsive. But she held it anyway.

"I'm here," she said. "I found you. And I'm not going anywhere."

She didn't know if Bree could hear her. Didn't know if it mattered. But she kept talking anyway—about their childhood, about their mother, about all the things that had happened in the four years they'd been apart. She talked until her voice went hoarse and the sun rose fully and the morning shift nurses came in to check on their patient.

She talked until Linda appeared in the doorway and gently suggested she get some rest.

"There's a hotel in town," Linda said. "You can come back during regular visiting hours. Stay as long as you need."

Celeste looked at Bree, who had returned to staring out the window at the trees.

"I'll be back," she said. "I promise. I'll be back every day until you remember me. Until you come back to me."

She kissed her sister's forehead—cold, still, like kissing marble—and walked out of the room.

The hotel was a small bed-and-breakfast on the main street of the nearest town—a place called Millbrook that seemed to consist entirely of a general store, a diner, and three churches. Celeste checked in, went to her room, and sat on the edge of the bed without taking off her jacket.

She should sleep. She should eat. She should call her mother and tell her that Bree was alive, that she'd found her, that there was still a chance.

Instead, she pulled out her phone and stared at the blank screen.

Maya Sharma. Mira. Whatever she called herself. The woman who had done this to Bree.

Celeste had left the studio without confronting her. Had driven through the night chasing the hope that her sister might still be saved. But now, sitting in this small room in this small town, she felt the rage building.

Bree was alive. But Bree was broken. Whatever Mira had taken from her—that essential thing, that center, that sense of self—it hadn't come back on its own in three and a half years. It might never come back.

And Maya—or Mira, or whoever was in control now—was still out there. Still free. Still capable of doing to others what she'd done to Bree.

Celeste needed answers. She needed to know if what was taken could be returned. She needed to understand how the hollowing worked, whether it could be reversed, what she would have to do to try.

She needed to go back.

But first, she needed to rest. Just for a few hours. Just enough to think clearly, to plan, to figure out her next move.

She lay down on the bed without undressing and closed her eyes.

She dreamed of her sister. Not the empty shell in the psychiatric facility, but the real Bree—laughing, alive, she dreamt of the silver sharpie coffee cup on the toe of her shoe.

Now we're connected, dream-Bree said. *No matter how far I go.*

I found you, Celeste replied. *I'm going to bring you back.*

Promise?

Promise.

When she woke, the sun was high in the sky and she knew what she had to do.

She was going back to the city. Back to the studio. Back to the woman who had stolen her sister's soul.

And she was going to get it back.

19

CHAPTER NINETEEN
Celeste
The Return

The drive back to the city felt longer than the drive out.

Celeste had stayed in Vermont for three days, visiting Bree every morning and every afternoon, sitting beside her sister's chair and talking until her voice gave out. Sometimes Bree seemed to hear her—a flicker in her eyes, a twitch of her fingers, a single word surfacing from the depths like a message in a bottle. *Coffee. Dork. Mom.* Once, on the second afternoon, Bree had turned to look at her and said, clear as day, *You came.*

Then the light had faded, and she'd gone away again.

But those moments—those tiny, flickering moments of recognition—were enough. Enough to prove that Bree was still in there. Enough to give Celeste hope that whatever had been taken might somehow be returned.

She'd talked to the doctors, the nurses, the specialists who had been treating Bree for three and a half years. None of them could explain what had happened to her. The brain scans showed no damage. The blood work showed no abnormalities.

Physically, Bree was healthy. But psychologically, she was a house with the lights turned off. Someone home, but barely.

"We've tried everything," Dr. Okonkwo, the staff psychiatrist, had told her. "Medication, therapy, electroconvulsive treatment. Nothing has made a significant difference. It's like she's missing something we can't identify—something that doesn't show up on any test we know how to run."

Her center, Celeste had thought. *The thing that made her Bree.*

"Is there any chance of recovery?" she'd asked.

Dr. Okonkwo had hesitated. "In cases like this, we usually see improvement in the first year if we're going to see it at all. After three and a half years..." She'd shaken her head slowly. "I don't want to give you false hope. But I also can't tell you it's impossible. The human mind is capable of remarkable things. Sometimes people come back from places we never expected them to return from."

"What would it take? What would help?"

"Connection. Familiarity. Things that anchor her to who she was before." Dr. Okonkwo had looked at her with kind, tired eyes. "You being here—that's the best thing that's happened to her since she arrived. Keep coming. Keep talking to her. Keep reminding her who she is."

So Celeste had kept coming. Had kept talking. Had held Bree's hand and shown her photographs and played songs from their childhood and told her stories about the life they'd shared.

And now she was driving back to the city, leaving her sister behind, because there was something she needed to do. Someone she needed to find.

Maya Sharma wasn't going to get away with this. Celeste would make sure of it.

The studio was closed when she arrived.

A handwritten sign on the door read: *Closed for personal emergency. Classes will resume next week. Namaste.*

Celeste tried the door anyway. Locked.

She peered through the windows, but the black fabric that had covered them on the night of her last visit had been removed. Inside, she could see the empty studio—mats stacked neatly against the wall, candles arranged on the altar, everything pristine and waiting.

Waiting for a teacher who wasn't coming back.

A woman walked past on the sidewalk, yoga mat slung over her shoulder. Celeste stopped her.

"Excuse me—do you know what's going on with the studio? When it's reopening?"

The woman's face fell. "You didn't hear? Maya's taking a sabbatical. Mental health reasons. She announced it a few days ago." She pulled out her phone and scrolled to Instagram. "Here—she posted about it."

Celeste looked at the screen.

A photograph of Maya silhouetted against a sunset, arms raised in a yoga pose. Beneath it, a caption:

Sometimes the teacher has to become the student again. I'm taking some time away to heal, to grow, to find my way back to myself. Thank you for holding space for me. I love you all.

The comments numbered in the thousands. Hearts, prayers, crying emojis. Messages of support and love and desperate pleas for her to come back soon.

"It's so sad," the woman said, taking her phone back. "She seemed so together, you know? Like nothing could ever touch her. I guess you never really know what someone's going through."

Celeste felt something cold settle in her stomach.

"When did she post this?"

"Three days ago. The morning after she taught her last

class." The woman shook her head sadly. "She told everyone in Power Vinyasa that she needed to step back. Half the class was crying. It was beautiful, actually—the way she was so honest about struggling. So vulnerable."

Three days ago. The same morning Celeste had arrived in Vermont.

She knew, Celeste thought. *She knew exactly when I'd be gone and how long I'd stay.*

"Do you know where she went?"

"No one does. She said she was going off the grid. Unplugging completely." The woman smiled wistfully. "Very on-brand for her, right? The wellness guru healing herself in silence."

Celeste thanked her and walked away, her mind racing.

Maya's apartment building was a high-rise on the Upper West Side. Doorman building. The kind of place that cost more per month than most people earned in a year.

Celeste had found the address during her initial investigation—cross-referencing property records, business filings, the paper trail that proved Maya Sharma existed and Mira Sharma didn't.

The doorman stopped her in the lobby. "Can I help you?"

"I'm here to see Maya Sharma. Apartment 1847."

"Ms. Sharma isn't in residence at the moment."

"When will she be back?"

The doorman's expression remained professionally neutral. "I'm not at liberty to say."

"I'm her assistant," Celeste lied smoothly. "From the studio. She asked me to check on something in her apartment while she's away. Pick up some documents she forgot."

The doorman studied her for a long moment. Then he picked up the phone and dialed.

"I'm calling the building manager. She'll need to verify—"

"That's fine. Call whoever you need to call." Celeste kept her voice calm, professional. "I'll wait."

Ten minutes later, she was riding the elevator to the eighteenth floor.

The building manager—a harried woman named Patricia—had been surprisingly easy to convince. Celeste had dropped enough details about the studio, about Maya's schedule, about the "documents related to the sabbatical announcement" to sound legitimate. And Patricia, clearly overwhelmed by the logistics of a high-profile tenant's sudden departure, had been happy to hand the problem to someone else.

"Just lock up when you're done," she'd said, pressing a master key into Celeste's hand. "And if you talk to Ms. Sharma, tell her we hope she feels better soon."

The hallway was carpeted in deep burgundy, the walls hung with tasteful art, the lighting soft and flattering. Everything about it whispered money and success and carefully curated perfection.

Apartment 1847 was at the end of the hall.

Celeste unlocked the door and stepped inside.

The apartment was beautiful. Floor-to-ceiling windows looking out over the city. Minimalist furniture in cream and gray. Fresh flowers on every surface—no, not fresh. Wilting slightly. Three days old, maybe four.

The same flowers that had been here when Maya left.

Celeste walked through the rooms slowly, looking for anything that might tell her where Maya had gone. The kitchen was spotless, the refrigerator empty except for condiments and a half-empty bottle of champagne. The bedroom was equally bare—closet half-empty, drawers cleaned out, no personal items on the nightstand.

She'd taken her time. Packed carefully. Left nothing behind that mattered.

The living room showed the same deliberate absence. No photographs on the walls. No books on the shelves. No papers on the desk—just a pristine surface, wiped clean of anything that might leave a trace.

Celeste checked the desk drawers anyway. Empty. She checked the filing cabinet in the corner. Empty. She checked the bathroom, the coat closet, the storage space behind the water heater.

Nothing. Nothing. Nothing.

Maya Sharma had erased herself from this apartment as thoroughly as if she'd never existed.

No, Celeste corrected herself. *Not Maya. Mira.*

Mira had done this. Mira had planned this. While Maya's face smiled for the cameras and Maya's voice reassured the students and Maya's hands signed the paperwork, Mira had been preparing to disappear.

And she'd timed it perfectly.

Three days. Celeste had been in Vermont for three days, sitting beside her broken sister, completely unaware that the woman she should have been watching was liquidating her life and vanishing into thin air.

She sank onto the cream-colored sofa and pressed her hands against her face.

She played me, she thought. *She played all of us.*

Her phone buzzed. A text from a number she didn't recognize.

Hope you found what you were looking for.

Celeste's blood went cold.

She typed back: *Where are you?*

The response came instantly: *Somewhere you'll never find me. Don't bother looking.*

You can't just disappear. Someone will recognize you.

Maya Sharma will disappear. Sabbatical turns into retirement. Retirement turns into seclusion. Seclusion turns into rumor, then memory, then nothing. It happens all the time. People forget.

Celeste stared at the screen, her fingers trembling.

I won't forget. I'll find you.

A long pause. Then:

No. You won't. Because you have a choice to make, Celeste. You can spend the rest of your life chasing a woman who no longer exists. Or you can go back to Vermont and save the sister who's still there.

You're a monster.

I'm a survivor. There's a difference.

Another pause. Then:

The technique takes. But connection can rebuild. Not what I took—that's gone forever. But something new. Something that might be enough.

I don't believe you.

You don't have to. But I've seen it happen. Some of them came back. Not all the way—never all the way—but enough. Enough to have lives again. Enough to remember who they loved and why.

Celeste felt tears running down her face.

Why are you telling me this?

Because I'm not completely heartless. And because I want you to stop looking for me. Go back to your sister. Be the connection she needs. Give her a reason to rebuild.

And if I don't? If I keep looking?

Then you'll waste years chasing a ghost while Bree sits in that chair by the window, waiting for someone to remind her who she is. Your choice.

The phone buzzed one more time.

Goodbye, Celeste. I hope she comes back to you. I genuinely do.

Then nothing. The number went dead—disconnected, probably a burner, untraceable.

Celeste sat in the empty apartment for a long time, staring at the screen, watching the sun set over the city through windows that framed a view Maya Sharma would never see again.

She could call the police. Could file a report, make accusations, try to start an investigation.

But what would she say? That a woman with a dissociative disorder had done something terrible to her sister using a breathing technique? That she'd "stolen her center"? That she'd "hollowed her out"?

No court would take it seriously. No prosecutor would touch it. There was no evidence of assault, no evidence of anything except a woman who'd had a mental breakdown at a yoga retreat and never recovered.

And while Celeste was fighting a legal battle she couldn't win, Bree would be sitting in that chair in Vermont. Waiting. Fading. Disappearing a little more each day.

The technique takes. But connection can rebuild.

She didn't want to believe it. Didn't want to accept anything that came from the woman who had destroyed her sister.

But Dr. Okonkwo had said the same thing. *Connection. Familiarity. Things that anchor her to who she was before.*

Maybe it was true. Maybe there was a chance.

Or maybe Mira was lying—manipulating her one last time, keeping her focused on Bree so she wouldn't keep looking.

It didn't matter.

Because even if it was a manipulation, even if there was no

chance of Bree ever coming back, Celeste knew what she had to do.

She had to try.

She stood up from the sofa and walked to the door. Paused at the threshold, looking back at the empty apartment one last time.

Maya Sharma had lived here. Had built an empire from this address, had touched thousands of lives, had been loved and admired and trusted by people who never knew what she really was.

And now she was gone. Vanished. Become someone else, somewhere else, probably already building a new life with a new name and new victims.

Celeste couldn't stop her. Couldn't find her. Couldn't make her pay for what she'd done.

But she could save Bree. Or try to. Or die trying.

She walked out of the apartment and closed the door behind her.

The drive back to Vermont took three hours and twenty-seven minutes.

This time, she didn't notice the miles passing. Didn't think about Maya or Mira or the woman who had become both and neither. Didn't think about justice or vengeance or the unfairness of a world where monsters got to disappear while their victims sat in psychiatric facilities, staring at nothing.

She thought about Bree.

About the sister she'd grown up with, the sister she'd fought with, the sister she'd loved even when loving her was hard. About coffee stains and silver Sharpies and a cartoon cup drawn on a shoe the last morning of their old life.

About the word *coffee*, surfacing from the depths of a broken mind like a message in a bottle.

About the whispered *you came*.

She was still in there. Somewhere. Buried under whatever Mira had taken, but still there.

And Celeste was going to find her.

Not by chasing a ghost across the world. Not by fighting battles she couldn't win. But by sitting beside her sister's chair, day after day, week after week, month after month. By talking until her voice gave out and then talking some more. By showing her photographs and playing her songs and telling her stories until something—anything—sparked behind those empty eyes.

By being the connection that might rebuild what had been destroyed.

It might not work. Probably wouldn't work. The doctors had said as much.

But Celeste was done calculating odds. Done weighing costs and benefits. Done being the journalist who always kept her distance, who never got too close, who observed and recorded but never really felt.

Bree was her sister. Her only sister. And she was going to fight for her with everything she had.

Whatever was left when the fight was over—that would be enough.

It would have to be.

She arrived at Pine Grove just as the sun was setting.

The facility looked different in the golden light—softer, somehow. Less like a place where broken people went to be forgotten and more like a place where they might, possibly, be found.

Celeste parked in the visitor lot and sat for a moment, watching the light fade over the mountains.

Then she got out of the car and walked inside.

Bree was where she'd left her. Same chair. Same window. Same distant stare at something only she could see.

But when Celeste sat down beside her and took her hand, Bree's fingers twitched. Moved. Wrapped around hers with the faintest pressure.

"Hey," Celeste said softly. "I'm back."

Bree didn't respond. Didn't turn. Didn't speak.

But she didn't let go of Celeste's hand, either.

And for now, that was enough.

20

CHAPTER TWENTY
Mira
The Beginning

Six months later.

The cliffs of New Zealand were everything she'd imagined and more.

She stood at the edge of the overlook, her hair loose around her shoulders, the wind pulling at the soft linen of her dress. Below her, the Tasman Sea churned against ancient rocks, sending plumes of white spray into the air. Above her, the sky stretched endless and blue, unmarked by clouds or planes or any sign of the world she'd left behind.

She was someone else now.

Not Maya Sharma, the wellness guru with forty-seven million TED Talk views. Not Mira, the shadow who handled things in the dark. Not even the nameless original who had shattered in a closet thirty-four years ago.

She was no one. And everyone. A woman without a name, standing on a cliff at the edge of the world, finally free of all the identities that had weighed her down.

The documents had been easy enough to acquire. The lawyer in New York had known people who knew people, and for the right price, a new person had been born—complete with a passport, a driver's license, a modest investment portfolio, and a clean history that would survive any background check.

Maya Sharma had sold everything. The studios, the supplement line, the intellectual property. She'd announced a sabbatical for "personal health reasons," and the wellness world had responded with an outpouring of support and concern. *Take care of yourself, Maya. We love you. Come back when you're ready.*

She wasn't coming back.

The money had been transferred to offshore accounts, then routed through a series of shells until it emerged clean and untraceable. Enough to live comfortably for the rest of her life. Enough to build something new.

She'd chosen New Zealand because it was far. Because it was beautiful. Because the accent was easy to adopt and the people were friendly and no one asked too many questions about why a woman might want to start over in her forties.

She'd rented a small house on the South Island, near Queenstown but not too near. A place with views of the mountains and easy access to hiking trails and a garden where she'd started growing vegetables, of all things. The domesticity of it amused her. Maya would have hired someone to tend a garden. Mira wouldn't have bothered with one at all.

But this new version of herself—this nameless woman who was both and neither—she liked getting her hands dirty. Liked the simple, physical satisfaction of planting seeds and watching them grow.

She liked a lot of things about this new life. The quiet. The anonymity. The freedom to be whoever she wanted to be, without the weight of an empire or the expectations of millions.

And she liked the hunger.

It was still there, of course. The void that had driven her to consume pieces of other people—it hadn't gone away just because she'd changed her location and shed her name. It was always there, gnawing at the edges of her consciousness, demanding to be fed.

But she'd learned to manage it. To find other sources of sustenance. The energy of a crowded café. The openness of tourists on vacation, their defenses down, their emotions close to the surface. She didn't take much—just a taste, here and there. Just enough to keep the hunger at bay without leaving anyone too damaged.

She was careful now. Controlled. She'd learned from the mistakes of her past life.

Celeste Park had taught her that.

She thought about the journalist sometimes, in the quiet hours of the evening when the sun set over the mountains and the world went soft and golden. Wondered if she'd gone back to Vermont. Wondered if she was sitting beside her sister's bed, reading to her, showing her photographs, trying to rebuild a person from fragments.

Wondered if it was working.

Part of her hoped it was. The Maya part, maybe—the soft part that had been pushed down into the darkness but never quite extinguished. That part wanted Bree to recover. Wanted Celeste to succeed. Wanted something good to come from all the damage that had been done.

But another part of her—the part that had survived, that had won, that was standing on this cliff in a new country with no name—that part didn't really care. Bree was a loose end from a previous life. Celeste was a threat that had been neutralized. Neither of them mattered anymore.

What mattered was this. The wind in her hair. The spray on

her face. The vast, indifferent beauty of a world that didn't know or care who she was.

She was free.

For the first time in thirty-four years, she was truly free.

The yoga studio opened three months later.

It was small—nothing like the empire Maya had built in New York. Just a single room in a converted barn on the outskirts of Queenstown, with bamboo floors and big windows and a hand-painted sign that read *Breathe & Be*.

She'd gotten the certification online, of course—Maya's decades of training more than qualified her, but her new identity needed paper credentials. Something to point to when people asked about her background.

The classes were popular. Tourists mostly, looking for something to do between bungee jumping and wine tours. But a few locals too—women from town, retired couples, a handful of young people searching for meaning in downward dog and warrior pose.

She taught gentle classes. Yin yoga. Restorative. Nothing too intense. Nothing that required the kind of heat and sweat and pushing through pain that Maya had been famous for.

Breathe & Be was about softness. About surrender. About letting go.

About trust.

She'd forgotten how good it felt to stand in front of a room full of people and guide them into stillness. To watch their faces relax, their shoulders drop, their breath slow and deepen. To feel them open up, layer by layer, until they were completely vulnerable. Completely present.

Completely hers.

She didn't take from them. Not much. Just the faintest sip, now and then, when the hunger got too strong to ignore. Just enough to keep herself fed without leaving marks.

They never noticed. They never did. They thought the lightness they felt after class was enlightenment, awakening, the natural result of an hour spent breathing and stretching.

They didn't know they'd given her something. They didn't know she'd taken.

And she was careful to make sure they never would.

Her name was Emma.

She came to the Thursday evening class for the first time in October, three months after the studio opened. Young—early twenties, maybe. Pretty in a fragile way, with dark circles under her eyes and a tremor in her hands that suggested she hadn't been sleeping well.

She set up her mat in the back corner, as far from the other students as possible. Kept her eyes down. Didn't make small talk.

She noticed her immediately.

Not because she was pretty. Not because she was fragile. But because of what she could feel radiating off her, even from across the room.

Need.

The girl was a wound walking. A black hole of loneliness and desperation and hunger for connection. The kind of person who would attach herself to anyone who offered warmth. The kind of person who would give everything she had for the promise of being seen.

The kind of person Mira used to target.

She watched her through the class. Watched her struggle

with the poses, her body stiff and uncooperative. Watched her fight back tears during the hip opener, the way so many people did when long-held tension finally started to release.

Watched her lie in savasana with her eyes squeezed shut, her whole body trembling with the effort of letting go.

After class, when the other students had rolled up their mats and drifted out into the evening, Emma stayed behind. She sat on her mat, hugging her knees to her chest, staring at nothing.

She approached slowly. "Are you okay?"

Emma looked up. Her eyes were wet. "I'm sorry. I don't know why I'm—I just—"

"It's okay." She sat down beside her, close but not too close. "Yoga brings things up sometimes. Emotions we've been holding onto without realizing it."

"I shouldn't have come. I'm a mess. I'm sorry."

"Don't apologize." Her voice was soft, warm, exactly the voice Maya used to use when she was cultivating a new student. "What's your name?"

"Emma."

"It's nice to meet you, Emma." She reached out and touched the girl's hand—just a brush of fingers, light and brief. "Do you want to talk about it?"

Emma shook her head. Then nodded. Then shook her head again.

"I just moved here," she said finally. "From Sydney. I was supposed to start a new job, but it fell through. And my boyfriend—" Her voice cracked. "My boyfriend didn't come with me. He was supposed to, but at the last minute, he said he couldn't. Said we needed a break. Said—"

She broke off, pressing her hands against her face.

She made sympathetic sounds. Patted her shoulder. Said all

the things a kind stranger would say to a broken girl in the back of a yoga studio.

And underneath the comfort, underneath the warmth, she felt something stir.

The hunger.

Emma was perfect. So broken, so needy, so desperate for someone to see her. She would give anything to feel less alone. She would trust anyone who offered kindness.

She would be so easy to consume.

She let the thought sit for a moment. Let herself imagine it: the synchronization, the deep relaxation, the moment of surrender when Emma breathed out and she breathed in. The rush of taking someone's center. The temporary fullness that followed.

Then she let the thought go.

Not because she felt guilty. Not because she'd suddenly developed a conscience. But because she was careful now. Controlled. She'd built a good life here, a quiet life, and she wasn't going to risk it for one feeding.

There would be others. There were always others. The world was full of broken people looking for someone to fix them.

She could afford to be patient.

"Emma," she said gently. "I want you to know that you're welcome here. Any time. No judgment, no expectations. Just a safe space to breathe."

Emma looked at her with wet, grateful eyes. "Really?"

"Really." She smiled—the warm, Maya smile, the one that made people feel like they'd finally found home. "Sometimes that's all we need. A place to breathe."

Emma nodded, wiping her tears. "Thank you. Thank you so much. I'll come back. I'll definitely come back."

"I hope you do."

She helped her to her feet, walked her to the door, watched her disappear into the evening.

Then she went back inside and began cleaning up the studio. Rolling mats, stacking blankets, straightening the altar with its singing bowls and candles.

Outside, the sun was setting over the mountains. The sky was painted in shades of orange and pink, the same colors it had been on that morning six months ago when she'd walked out of Maya's apartment and become someone new.

She paused at the window, looking out at the fading light.

Somewhere in Vermont, Celeste Park was probably sitting beside her sister's bed, reading to her, talking to her, trying to rebuild a person from fragments.

Somewhere in New Jersey, Sunita Sharma was probably staring at a phone that would never ring, waiting for a daughter who no longer existed.

Somewhere in the darkness at the back of her own mind, Maya was probably still screaming—if she was still conscious at all.

But here, in this small studio on the edge of the world, she was at peace.

She had everything she needed. A new life, a steady supply of broken people looking for guidance. The hunger was fed. The void was filled. The endless ache of emptiness that had driven her for thirty-four years was finally, blissfully quiet.

She was free.

She was whole.

She was home.

And somewhere in the back of the studio, where a young woman named Emma had just started her journey toward destruction, a new story was beginning.

. . .

The End.

Or is it?

Yes! Perfect setup for a sequel. Here's a revised epilogue that plants those seeds:

EPILOGUE
Vermont
One Year Later

The room was bright with afternoon sunlight.

Bree sat in her chair by the window, the same chair she'd been sitting in when Celeste first found her. But something was different now. Her posture was straighter. Her eyes were clearer. Her hands, resting in her lap, were still instead of trembling.

"Do you remember the time we tried to make Mom's birthday cake?" Celeste asked. She was sitting beside the window, a photo album open on her lap. "You put salt in instead of sugar. The whole thing was completely inedible."

Bree's lips curved. Not quite a smile—she still didn't smile, not really—but something close.

"Salt," she said. The word came out slowly, carefully, like she was tasting it. "I remember. Mom tried to eat it anyway."

"She did. She took one bite and her whole face puckered, but she didn't want to hurt your feelings. She said—"

"'It's very... unique.'" Bree's voice was stronger now. Clearer. "That's what she said. 'Very unique.'"

Celeste felt tears prick at her eyes. She blinked them back. She'd learned not to cry in front of Bree—not because it upset her, but because Bree always tried to comfort her, and the effort exhausted her.

"You're doing so well," she said instead. "The doctors are amazed."

"The doctors don't understand." Bree turned to look at her, and for a moment—just a moment—she looked exactly like the sister Celeste remembered. Sharp. Present. Herself. "They think I'm recovering. But I'm not recovering. I'm building."

"Building?"

"A new me. From pieces." Bree's hand moved to her chest, pressing against the place where her heart beat. "The old Bree is gone. You know that. Whatever that woman took from me—it's never coming back."

Celeste nodded. She'd accepted that months ago, after reading through the folder Maya had given her. The center, once taken, was gone forever. There was no reversing it.

"But I can make something new," Bree continued. "From the pieces that are left. From the memories you bring me, the stories you tell me, the—" She paused, searching for the word. "The love. From the love."

"Is it enough?"

Bree was quiet for a long moment.

"Ask me again in a year," she said finally. "Or five. Or ten. I don't know yet what I'm becoming. I just know that I'm becoming something. And that's more than I had before."

Celeste reached out and took her sister's hand. It was warm now, where it had once been cold. Alive.

"I'll keep bringing you pieces," she said. "For as long as it takes."

"I know." Bree squeezed her hand. "That's why I'm still here."

They sat in comfortable silence for a while, watching the

trees sway outside the window. The afternoon light shifted, shadows lengthening across the floor.

"You're still looking for her," Bree said quietly. It wasn't a question.

Celeste stiffened. "What makes you say that?"

"I'm broken, not blind." Bree's voice held a ghost of her old sharpness. "I see the way you check your phone. The way you disappear for hours and come back with that look on your face. The folder you think I don't know about—the one you keep in your bag."

Celeste didn't deny it. She'd been carrying the folder everywhere for months—the list of thirty-seven names, the notes on the technique, the patterns she'd started to identify. The breadcrumbs she'd been following across the internet, searching for any sign of a woman who had vanished into thin air.

"She's still out there," Celeste said. "Somewhere. And she's not going to stop. People like her don't stop."

"So you're going to find her?"

"I'm going to try." Celeste's jaw tightened. "I've been in contact with some of the others. The ones on her list who recovered enough to talk. There's a woman in Arizona—Vera Chen—she's been tracking patterns for years. Strange clusters of psychological breaks in wellness communities. Yoga retreats where people check in healthy and check out hollow. It's not just Maya. Vera thinks she might have taught others. Or inspired them."

Bree was quiet for a long moment.

"That's dangerous," she said finally. "What she does—what she did to me—you can't fight that with research and phone calls."

"I know."

"She'll come for you if you get too close. She'll do to you what she did to me."

"Maybe." Celeste met her sister's eyes. "But I spent four years searching for you without knowing what I was looking for. Now I know. Now I understand how she operates, how she chooses her victims, how she hides. And I have something I didn't have before."

"What?"

Celeste pulled a small notebook from her bag. It was worn, the pages filled with her cramped handwriting—names, dates, locations, patterns. A year's worth of obsessive documentation.

"A map," she said. "Of everywhere she's been. Everyone she's hurt. The techniques she uses, the warning signs, the way she builds trust before she feeds." She flipped to a page near the back. "And I have this."

She held up a printout—a photograph, grainy but clear enough. A small yoga studio with big windows and a hand-painted sign. *Breathe & Be.*

"Where is that?" Bree asked.

"New Zealand. South Island, near Queenstown. The business was registered eight months ago. The woman who runs it matches Maya's description—same age, same build, same teaching style. She appeared out of nowhere with credentials that don't quite check out."

"That could be anyone."

"It could be." Celeste tucked the photograph back into the notebook. "But three weeks ago, a young woman in Queenstown was admitted to a psychiatric facility. Twenty-three years old. No history of mental illness. She'd been taking yoga classes at a small studio outside of town. Her family says she came back from a retreat and wasn't the same. They say it was like something essential had been removed."

Bree's face went pale. "She's doing it again."

"She never stopped." Celeste's voice was hard. "And she won't stop. Not unless someone stops her."

"Celeste..." Bree's grip on her hand tightened. "Promise me you'll be careful. Promise me you won't let her take you too."

"I promise." Celeste leaned forward and kissed her sister's forehead. "I'm not going to let her win. Not after everything she's taken. Not after what she did to you."

She stood and walked to the window, looking out at the Vermont hills rolling green and gold in the late afternoon light.

"There are others out there," she said quietly. "Other people like you—hollowed out, abandoned, left to rot in facilities where no one knows who they were or what happened to them. The ones on her list, plus who knows how many more she never bothered to document. They deserve to be found. They deserve to have someone fight for them the way I fought for you."

"You can't save everyone."

"No." Celeste turned back to face her sister. "But I can try. And I can make sure she never does this to anyone else."

Bree studied her for a long moment. Then, slowly, she nodded.

"The folder," she said. "The one in your bag. There's a name in there—Diana Reyes. She was hollowed in 2019. I remember her from... from when I was inside. From the dark place. I felt her there, sometimes. Like an echo."

Celeste frowned. "You felt her?"

"We're connected. The ones she broke. I don't know how to explain it, but..." Bree pressed her hand to her chest again. "There's a thread. Faint, but there. Like we're all missing the same piece, and somewhere in the dark, those missing pieces are still touching."

"That's..." Celeste didn't have words for what that was.

"Find Diana," Bree said. "She was a psychiatrist before it happened. If anyone understands what she did to us—how she did it—it's Diana."

"Do you know where she is?"

"No. But I know she's still alive. I can feel her." Bree's eyes were distant now, focused on something Celeste couldn't see. "She's getting stronger. Like me. Building herself back, piece by piece."

Celeste pulled out her notebook and wrote the name down. *Diana Reyes. Psychiatrist. 2019. Connected.*

"Thank you," she said. "This helps."

"Just promise me one thing."

"Anything."

Bree's gaze sharpened, focusing on Celeste with an intensity that hadn't been there a year ago. An intensity that was entirely new.

"When you find her—when you find the woman who did this to me—don't try to save her. Don't try to understand her. Don't give her a chance to explain or apologize or make you feel sorry for her." Bree's voice was cold. Harder than Celeste had ever heard it. "Just stop her. Whatever it takes. Whatever it costs. Make sure she never breathes anyone in again."

Celeste held her sister's gaze.

"I will," she said. "I promise."

Outside the window, the sun was beginning to set. The trees cast long shadows across the lawn, and somewhere in the distance, a bird was singing.

But Celeste wasn't thinking about the beauty of the evening. She was thinking about a studio in New Zealand, a woman with no name, and a young girl named Emma who had no idea what was coming for her.

She was thinking about the hunt.

It would take time. It would take resources she didn't have yet and connections she hadn't made. It would mean leaving Bree, at least temporarily, and that thought hurt more than she wanted to admit.

But she'd spent four years searching for her sister without knowing what she was looking for.

Now she knew exactly what she was hunting.

And this time, she wouldn't stop until she found it.

The End.

Made in the USA
Coppell, TX
15 February 2026

72017951R10115